Jase

KINGS OF KORRUPTION

novel

by

GERI GLENN

Jase is a work of fiction. Names, characters, places, and incidents are the products of the author's imagination and are used fictitiously. Any resemblance to actual events, locales, or persons, living or dead, is entirely coincidental.

Cover Art
Wicked by Design

Editing
Rebel Edit & Design

Formatting
Tracey Jane Jackson
www.traceyjanejackson.com

2016 Geri Glenn
Copyright © 2016 by Geri Glenn
All rights reserved.

ISBN-13: 978-1530867899
ISBN-10: 1530867894

Published in the United States

Acknowledgements

Let's see if I can get everyone in…so many people made this possible and I'm sure I'll miss someone.

To My Kids – You can't read this book until you're at least 35, but when you do, you can read here just how grateful I am to both of you. You put up with my long hours and crazy hair after a long day of trying to find the words, and continue to tell me I'm pretty and not insane. Thank you for being the most amazing girls a mom could ask for.

To Christina DeRoche – What would I do without you? You are an incredible support to me when I am writing, and these books would never turn out right without our giggling brainstorming sessions, or your unbridled honesty. So excited to hit New Orleans with you in a few months.

To Jacqueline Sinclair – You are my sounding board, my most trusted beta and my friend. Thank you for your friendship and your help. I look forward to meeting you some day. Til then, we'll always have the Riviera …

To Tracey Jackson – You are one hard lady to please, and I wouldn't have you any other way! Thank you for the last minute save. I count myself lucky to call you friend.

To Amanda DiPierro – You spend an incredible amount of time promoting the shit out of these books, and for that, I thank you. You are a wonderful PA, and I'm lucky to have found you.

To Johnna Siebert – Thank you for all that you do to help me get my books out there. You are an amazing PA, and a wonderful friend!

To Nicole Lloyd – I am proud to say that you are my pimp. I love all the tags I get, showing me just how hard you work, just because you're awesome! You have been there at a moments notice to Beta read for me and give opinion, and are a friend that I value greatly.

To The Girls at Night Owl Author Services – You ladies have been incredible. I love the posts and pictures I see you all posting, and you have made an incredible difference in my writing time. Thanks to you, I can focus more on writing, and less on promoting because I know you have my back.

To Rebel Edit & Design – Dana, what did I ever do before you? You are the most thorough editor I've ever seen. I love how you take my rough work and turn it into something I can be proud of. Thank you for direction, your corrections, and your amazing ideas to make the whole thing better.

To Robin at Wicked by Design – Another cover, another hit. You are an amazing designer, and as usual, I love what you have done. Can't wait to see what the rest are going to look like!

To The Awesome Ladies at Saints & Sinners Book Promotions – Thank you once again for another successful release blitz. You ladies make my life so much easier at release time! Never stop doing what you do.

To My Groupies – You ladies are so much fun! You keep me sane, share my posts and make me laugh. Best fan group ever!

To The Bloggers – Everyone of you that took the time out of your busy schedule to post, review and/or talk about my books, thank you. A million times thank you! An indie author needs you amazing people to find readers, and I've been blessed to have so many of you support me.

And lastly, To The Readers – For every one of you that took a chance on me and bought my book, thank you! For those that left a review, double thank you! It's readers like you that give me the courage to keep writing, and improving my skill, hoping to bring you the best story I can. I thank all of you for making it possible to live my dream of writing full time. For any of you that have spread the word and shared my posts or told someone about my books, you keep me going! I love each and every one of you for whatever support you've given me! Thank you, thank you, thank you!

This book is for Brianna

The beginning of Ellen's journey, though not originally intended, largely became based on you. As a teenage mother, you have shown incredible maturity, resourcefulness and love. I am so overwhelmingly proud of the woman you have become. Evelyn is a lucky little girl. Love you kiddo.

Jase

12 Years Earlier

YANKING OPEN THE door of the gas station bathroom, I let the ladies walk out ahead of me. I follow them into the parking lot, checking my zipper to make sure it's up.

Whistles and catcalls ring through the air, coming from the bunch of grown-ass men on motorcycles to my left. I lean over and place my hand on the ass of each girl and kiss them one at a time.

"Ladies, it's been a pleasure meeting you."

They both giggle and toss a little wave over their shoulders as they walk back to their car, parked on the other side of the lot. I enjoy every step they take, watching their asses sway back and forth inside their cut-off jean shorts.

Once they're both inside their car, I turn towards my brothers and my waiting bike with a grin that I don't bother hiding. Why would I? Those girls were fucking hot. How many guys can say they've had a random threesome with two hot women they met at a gas station in the middle of nowhere?

I'm just swinging my leg over my ride when I hear my buddy, Ryker. "You're fuckin' unbelievable, man. Leave it to you to pick up some pussy on a deserted fuckin' highway."

"Jealous, fucker?" Soft chuckles from some of the others fill the air and my grin widens. I can't resist the urge to tease Ryker. "Hear that guys? Ryk's jealous 'cause he can't get no pussy."

"Oh, I can get pussy," he retorts, chucking an empty chocolate bar wrapper at me. "Every one of us can get pussy." He sweeps his arm out to indicate our brothers. Eleven gruff and burly bikers stand beside their motorcycles, shaking their heads and laughing at our exchange. It's nothing they haven't heard before.

Ryker and I grew up in their shadows, making a playground of their clubhouse. Our fathers were members of the Kings of Korruption Motorcycle Club long before we came along. They've listened to Ryker and me since we were just kids, running around, causing all kinds of shit. Now that we're finally fully patched members of the Kings ourselves, they get to hear it on their road trips too.

"The rest of us just know better than to stick our dick into any willing pussy there is," he continues. "We have fuckin' standards, man."

I frown and jerk my head back in confusion. "What do you mean 'standards?' Those girls were hot!" Ryker laughs and shakes his head. I roll my eyes. "Whatever, man. You wish you could get half the pussy I get."

"You're nineteen, Jase." I hear from behind me. I turn to see Smokey staring at me, eyes serious, as he takes a long haul off his cigarette. "For fuck's sake. Your pecker's gonna fall off before you even figure out how to use it properly."

I smile and cup my balls as laughter erupts from the group. "Fuck you, old man. I can fuck better than you, make the girls scream my name ten times louder than you ever could. We all know it."

He smirks and takes one final haul before tossing the butt to the pavement, crushing it beneath the toe of his giant boot. "Yeah, I'm sure you're a real fuckin' porn star, boy." He settles himself on his bike and points one of his big meaty fingers in my direction. "One of these days, Jase, you're gonna meet a bitch that won't let you sweet talk your way into her panties. You're gonna tie yourself up in fuckin' knots, tryin' to figure out a way in, but you're not gonna know how because you always pick the easy ones. You've never had to work for it."

I look to Ryker, who's standing by his bike with a giant grin on his face. He loves to see me catch hell from Smokey. "Apparently, Smokey missed the memo."

"Oh yeah? What memo's that?"

"The one that says what every one of these fuckers already know. That all women fuckin' love me."

Ellen

"It's positive," Julie says, her eyes wide as she holds up the white stick displaying the two pink lines.

My head swims as I gape at her in horror—my whole world seeming to screech to a halt. I open my mouth, but all I can manage is a choked gasp as I reach for the pregnancy test with a trembling hand. Hot tears fill my eyes, blurring my vision as I stare down at the test that may mean the end of every dream I've ever had for my future.

I have a baby growing inside of me—a real baby. I can't be a mom. Babies need stuff like milk, diapers, and a roof over their heads. I can't provide that...can I? How can I teach this baby any-thing when I'm still trying to figure life out for myself?

I lift my head and look at Julie, my chin trembling as a tear slips down my cheek. "What am I going to do?" My voice comes out in a terrified whisper as I struggle to catch my breath. I feel like I've been punched in the stomach.

I just turned sixteen! I have to finish high school and go to col-lege. I've worked so hard and get good grades because I want to be a doctor, but how would that be possible if I have a baby!

Julie wraps her arms around my shoulders and squeezes me tight. "Don't worry, El," she coos. "We'll figure this out." I cry as the feeling of hopelessness threatens to pull me under. Julie rocks me slowly from side to side as sobs wrack my entire body. I hold her as if my life depends on it, my tears soaking into her shirt. We stay that way for what feels like forever, and it's more than okay with me. The longer we stay in this bathroom, the longer I can avoid facing this problem.

Once my sobs subside and my breathing returns to normal, Julie lets me go and wipes at my cheeks with cheap toilet paper. "Class is just about to end," she whispers. "You need to tell Paul."

Again, my chest starts to tighten. *Paul.* He's not going to be happy. I've only been dating him for a couple of months now. He's eighteen, good looking, and captain of our school's football team. He's popular, and before him, I was not. I had friends, of course, but nothing compared to what I have now that Paul and I are together. When he'd shown an interest in me at the beginning of the school year, I'd been flattered. He'd asked me out on a Friday, and that very night, I went on my first date and had my first kiss. It was magical.

Things with Paul had moved fast, but I love him…at least I *think* I do. I know I would do anything for him, and that's why the idea of telling him about this has me wanting to barricade myself inside our high school bathroom until the end of time.

Julie holds her hand out, gesturing for me to take it. I stare at it, not wanting to take another step. I don't want to go out there, and I don't want to tell Paul. I don't want to be pregnant.

Julie waves her hand at me once more. I take a deep breath before grasping it like a lifeline. She leads me out of the bathroom and down the deserted hallway that will fill up with thousands of students as soon as the bell rings.

We turn the corner to go to my locker just as it rings. Students spill out of every door, clogging up the hallways, making me panic.

"Here he comes," Julie whispers. "I gotta get some stuff out of my locker. You talk to him and I'll meet you back here in a few minutes." She doesn't wait for an answer because Paul is already behind me.

His arm wraps around my waist and his lips graze the sensitive skin on the side of my neck. "Hey, babe."

I take a deep breath and straighten my shoulders, deciding that it's now or never. I could wait to tell him, but what's the point? I don't need to go through this alone if we can go through it together. We need to be a team.

I turn in his arms and paste on the best smile I can manage. "Hey."

His eyes narrow, not missing the fact that I'm acting strange. "What's going on?"

"Um…" I bite my lip and look around, making sure nobody is close enough to hear our conversation. "I need to talk to you." I stare up at him, doing my best to tell him with my eyes that this is serious.

"So talk."

I shuffle from foot to foot, my eyes not quite meeting his. "Well, I…" I take another deep breath and look at him from beneath my lashes. "This is important, and I'd like to talk to you in private."

His arm pulls away from me and he takes a step back, more than a little annoyed now as he looks me up and down. "What the fuck, Ellen? I've gotta get to practice, so just say what you gotta fuckin' say."

I taste blood on my tongue from nibbling furiously on my lower lip. Why is he being so mean? My eyes dart around the hall once more, not even taking in my surroundings anymore. My heart races, and I wish more than anything that the cement floor would open up and swallow me whole.

"I don't think this is—"

"Say it!" he snaps, not even caring who's listening.

My face heats as the chatter in the hall dulls. I look to see everyone within hearing distance watching us. I feel the bile rise up my throat as I take in his uncaring face. Suddenly, my fear is much different than just upsetting him. My fear is that he will abandon me altogether, and with everyone listening. Everyone will know.

I spin on my heel, intending to dash down the hall, but he grabs my arm and yanks me back. "What the fuck do you have to say that's so goddamn important?" I stare up at him, unable to believe that he would grab me like this. My arm hurts from where his fingers are digging into my flesh. "Whatever," he spits, shoving me away. "I don't have time for this shit."

"She's pregnant, you asshole," Julie says angrily from behind me. "Did I seriously just see you grab her?" My eyes are glued to Paul's, whose are wide now, and on me.

"This true?"

I nod, tears spilling down my cheeks.

"You saying it's mine?" he asks with his nostrils flared and his jaw clenched.

I can't believe he's asking me this. He's the only guy I've ever been with, and he knows that. He shakes his head from side to side, not bothering to hide the disgust on his face. "Yeah? Well, we'll see about that, you stupid bitch."

I watch in horror as he spins around and storms off down the hall. What just happened? Paul's never talked to me this way before.

A ninth grader with a large stack of books is in Paul's path. I cry out as he picks the kid off the ground, books and all, and tosses him against a locker. The poor boy slides to the ground, looking scared to death. Paul then pushes and shoves his way through the crowd, screaming at kids who are unfortunate enough to be in his way.

The hall erupts once more in a cacophony of conversation. I turn to face Julie, feeling even more afraid than I did before. "Well," she says, "that went well."

Jase

I STUFF MY dick back into my pants, yank up the zipper, and look down at the bitch on her knees. She looks up at me, licking her swollen lips as she starts to stand. Leaning forward, she smashes her mouth onto mine, slipping her tongue inside. Tasting myself is not something I enjoy, but I kiss her back. After all, she did suck my dick, so what's a kiss?

I'd met Tammy…Tania? Wait a minute…Tracy? Oh hell, whatever. About an hour ago, while I was playing pool with some of the guys, she'd walked up to me, slipped her hand in my back pocket, and told me I had a nice ass. The bitch is observant. I do have a nice ass.

I'd managed to finish my beer and another round of pool before she grabbed my hand and dragged me back here to the ladies' room. I wasn't going to argue. She pressed me back against the wall, unzipped my pants, and proceeded to allow me to blow off some steam. It was a win–win for the both of us.

I break our kiss and smile down at her. "You want another beer?"

"Hell yeah."

Snagging her hand, I lead her out of the dingy bathroom and into the main part of the bar. I order us each a beer and look around the room, seeing several of my brothers scattered throughout as they drink, laugh, and dance.

The Kings of Korruption Motorcycle Club has a clubhouse not far from here, complete with a fully stocked bar and a kick-ass speaker system. We spend a lot of time there, preferring to stick together and amongst our own people. But every once in a while, we need to branch out and meet some new bitches, get in a few brawls, and unwind. At least we don't have to worry about cleaning up our messes.

It's no mystery why we picked the Pig's Ear as our hangout. The tables and stools are ancient, covered in burn marks, and beaten-up with shit scratched into every surface. There are five pool tables off to the side that are well-maintained and always in use. The music is loud, and the local bitches come here in droves, always ready for a good time.

"You wanna dance?" Tammy asks, batting her heavily made-up eyelashes.

I turn to look at her, but my eyes land on a familiar face. "Nah, you go ahead, baby. I'm gonna go talk to my buddy for a minute."

Her lip pops out in a phony pout before she spins away, swaying her hips to the beat of the music as she walks to the dance floor. I watch her go, fully enjoying the flash of red panties I see beneath her short skirt.

Moving across the room, I come up behind Ryker and clap my hand down on his shoulder. "Hey, fucker."

"Jase."

I look around the table, smiling at everyone I see until my eyes land on a pair of brown ones that I haven't seen in months. *Ellen*. She stares back at me, her eyes wide, and I feel frozen in place. It's like time stops, and neither one of us are able to look away. The loud music and drone of voices fade to a faint background noise, drowned out by the beating of my own heart.

"Hi, Jase."

I blink and turn my head, focusing on the voice calling my name. Ryker's old lady, Charlie, stares back at me, her eyes narrowed and her mouth tight. Shit. Charlie's been giving me a hard time for months about Ellen, demanding I stay away from her, and I have. It's been easy because I never see her, but now that I have, it makes it a lot more difficult.

I try to hide my feelings as I grin at her. "Charles. I didn't see you over there."

Her mouth twists into a smirk. "Clearly."

I ignore her comment and greet everyone at the table, one by one. Reaper, Laynie, and Tease all sit back with huge smiles on their faces, but are quick to return my greeting. These fuckers know how into Ellen I am, and they're thoroughly enjoying this.

I'd first met Ellen at the palliative care home where she works with Charlie. We'd put Smokey in there when his battle with lung cancer was coming to an end. Smokey had been like a father to me and Ryk in a lot of ways, and had been a member of the Kings since the very beginning. Ellen had been one of the nurses that took care of him in those final days. I'd been attracted to her then, but she was always quick to make herself appear uninterested.

I'd only seen her one other time since Smokey had passed away, and that was here, at this very bar, just a few months ago. I'd tried to talk to her then, but Charlie had been all over me to stay away from her girl, but seeing her here tonight, I decide that Charlie can kiss my ass.

When my eyes meet hers once more, I clear my throat and smile. "Hey, Ellen."

I watch her cheeks flame and hear her quick intake of breath. "Hi, Jase."

I can tell just by looking at her that she's interested. Why the hell is Charlie cockblocking me? Moving closer to her, I turn my body to face her and lean against the table. "Haven't seen you in a while. You look…" I look her up and down, making damn sure she knows that I like what I see, "gorgeous. As always."

She raises her brow and her lip tips up on one side. "Does that line actually work on women?"

My brow furrows. "What line? That wasn't a line." I motion towards her. "You look fuckin' hot, woman."

Her cheeks flame brighter, and a choked laugh escapes her lips. "Well, thank you."

I stare into her smiling brown eyes, and neither of us say a word. I know we must look ridiculous, but I don't give a shit. I can't stop looking at the way her eyes crinkle in the corners when she laughs, or the way she's looking at me right now.

A body slams into mine from behind, then a pair of arms wrap themselves around my waist. "There you are. I've been looking all over for you."

I watch the smile fall from Ellen's face and the crinkles around her eyes smooth out as she looks over my shoulder. Turning, I paste on a fake smile and pull out of the unwanted embrace, taking my intruder by the hand so I can move her away from Ellen. "Everyone, meet Tammy."

I don't want them to meet Tammy. I want Tammy to disappear. I want that happy look back on Ellen's face.

She yanks her hand from mine and narrows her eyes at me. "It's Tawney. How is it you let me suck your dick five fucking minutes ago, but you can't even remember my damn name?"

Shit. "Tawney…right! That's what I—"

The sound of her open hand striking my cheek is barely heard over the noisy din of the bar, but everyone at that table hears it. Before I know it, Tawney's gone, and everyone's staring at me. They're all silent for a beat, but then they all burst into laughter.

I lock eyes with Ellen, who isn't laughing. It's quite the opposite, she looks disgusted.

Raising my hand, I press it to my lip and check for blood, but there is none. The only thing wounded here is my pride, and most likely, my shot with Ellen.

"Looks like you pissed Tammy off," Ryker chokes out through his wheezing laughter.

"Fuckin' priceless," Reaper snorts. "First time I ever saw a bitch pissed at you, Jase. It's like fuckin' Christmas!"

The three of them continue to cackle like a bunch of hyenas while I grit my teeth. Fuck them. This shit isn't funny. I look over to Charlie, and the disappointment on her face makes my stomach tighten. Then I look back to Ellen, but she avoids meeting my eyes.

"I'm gonna grab another beer." I walk away, thankful for any excuse to distance myself from them. *Fuck.* That bitch totally fucked up any chance I might have had with Ellen tonight. And what the fuck did she hit me for? I've never been slapped like that, ever.

Shaking my head, I order my beer and wade back through the sea of people to Ryker's table.

The first thing I notice is the empty seat. I look to Charlie, who just shakes her head and looks away.

For the first time in my life, a feeling I've never felt before threatens to overwhelm me. I slump down onto Ellen's abandoned stool, which is still warm, and my face heats as I realize what that feeling is.

Shame.

Looking up, my eyes meet Ryker's. He's watching me closely, fully aware that I'm upset. Well, fuck that, and fuck everyone else too. I didn't do anything wrong.

What's so bad about having a good time? Grinning, I shrug my shoulders and raise my glass.

No need to get worked up over it anyway. What's done is done.

Ellen

I toss the phone onto the couch with enough force that it bounces right off and onto the floor, the backing and battery pack scattering in opposite directions. *Damn it!* They should have been here two hours ago. I knew this was a bad idea.

This is the first time that my eleven-year-old son, Bryce, has ever had an overnight visit with his father. Paul had not been happy to find out I was pregnant and had ignored me up until about a year ago. Bryce had just turned ten when Paul met him.

I don't know why Paul suddenly came around, wanting to get to know Bryce, but who was I to turn away a father figure for my son? It's only been me and Bryce from the very beginning. After my parents had found out I was pregnant, they'd tried to force me into getting an abortion. When I refused, they'd turned their backs on me. They kicked me out of their house, telling me to never come back, and I damn well never did.

Thank God for my friend, Julie, and her parents. They'd taken me in, helped me get on my feet, and taught me all the right ways to be a parent. But they moved away a few years later, and even though Julie and I are still great friends, she lives in Toronto now. We see each other a few times a year, but that's it.

About a year ago, Paul had looked me up on Facebook and sent me a message, saying he would like a chance to get to know our son. I didn't know what to say. I've never lied to Bryce, and he always knew that his father was out there, but that we were teenagers when he was born, and his father wasn't ready for that kind of responsibility. Bryce had always taken that for what it was, and never asked questions.

I was worried that if I let Paul come around, after a while, he'd lose interest. How would that affect my boy? Or what if he decided that he wanted joint custody of Bryce? I couldn't deal with that. Every decision I've ever made, since the moment I saw those two pink lines on that pregnancy test, has been for him.

I'd reluctantly agreed, and we'd taken things pretty slow; slower than Paul wanted to take it. Over the past few months, I've let Paul take him out of my home, unsupervised. We started off with trips to the park, or lunches at McDonald's. Last night was their first overnighter, and I've been a wreck since the moment his big F-350 pulled out of my driveway.

Bryce has never stayed anywhere overnight besides his friend Jimmy's, whose mother I know and trust. For the first couple of hours after they left, I got some housework done. Then I tried to relax, but I couldn't. The house was too quiet. That's when I'd called Charlotte, or Charlie, which is the name everyone calls her by. She'd suggested I meet her at the Pig's Ear and take advantage of having a night to myself. I'd taken her up on it, just to get my mind off of whether or not Bryce had eaten a decent supper, or remembered to brush his teeth before bed.

Looking back, I wish I'd never gone. Part of me went because I knew Jase would be there. He's easily the most gorgeous man I've ever seen. He's also very flirty, which does wonders for my neglected ego. I've never had any intentions of pursuing him, but we'd had a moment last night, however brief it was.

When his date had practically attacked him from behind, immediately ending our moment, I could tell he was embarrassed—especially when he'd forgotten her name. Who the hell forgets the name of the girl they're with? When she began talking about their little hook up in the bathroom, Jase's eyes were on me, and I'd watched the blood drain from his face.

It had felt like a slap to the face. I don't even know why I'd been so bothered by it, or why I'm still bothered by it now. I had a pretty good idea of what kind of guy Jase was, but the proof being right in front of me was more than I could handle. She'd slapped him, and he deserved it, but I found myself wanting to claw her eyes out for it.

So the first chance I got, I left. I just wanted to be alone. I was tired. I'd always thought that the Kings of Korruption were cool and mysterious, but now that I've gotten to know a few of them, I realize that they're just regular people, and Jase is just a player. I haven't allowed myself to be played since Paul all those years ago, and I'll never let it happen again.

The front door slams against the wall as Bryce bustles in, carrying his backpack and a giant red foam finger. "Check it out, Mom. We went to the hockey game last night!"

I raise my eyes to see Paul coming in behind him, a wide smile on his face as he watches his son. Looking back to Bryce, I force a smile. "That's awesome, Bud. Sounds like you had fun." I reach out and tousle his hair as he beams up at me. "Why don't you take your stuff to your room? I need to talk to your dad alone for a minute."

The smile fades from Paul's face and his eyes narrow. "Okay," he says slowly, giving me a look that can't be mistaken for anything other than what it is—a warning.

Once Bryce is in his room, I turn to Paul. "Why didn't you answer my call? I was worried sick!"

His body straightens and he barks out an amused laugh, but I don't miss the angry edge to it. "Jesus, Ellen," he snaps. "We were having a good time, even *with* the phone ringing every five goddamn minutes. You need to cut the cord, woman. You're smothering the kid."

I jerk my head up. "Is that so?" I struggle to keep the anger I feel from making my voice quiver. I lift my arm and point down the hall towards Bryce's room. "That little boy down there, the one you say I'm smothering? He's eleven-years-old, Paul. I've been taking care of him all by myself his entire life, without any help from you." He sighs and opens his mouth to interrupt, but I continue, "Sometimes, in the middle of the night, he still has nightmares. When that happens, I go into his room and play with his hair and help him think of something happy to replace the scary images in his head."

Paul closes his mouth and stares at me. "Last week he fell off his bike and scraped up his shin. He came into the house, bloody and crying, and the only thing that could calm him down was a hug from his mom. He's a little boy, Paul. You can't even come close to knowing him as well as you think you do. So, I suggest you keep your parenting tips to yourself, until you've actually spent a lot more time being one."

His eyes narrow until they're nothing but slits, glaring daggers in my direction. He closes the space between us in an instant, grabbing my upper arm roughly. His fingers squeeze and dig into my skin through the sleeve of my shirt. I don't even have a chance to react before I hear Bryce bustle back into the room.

"Mom! Did you get tha—" His eyes widen and lock onto the place where his father grips my arm. "What's going on?"

Paul releases me and takes a step back. "Nothing, buddy. Your mom and I were just talking." He walks over to Bryce, giving his shoulder a squeeze. "I gotta go. Talk to you later, okay?"

Bryce nods, and without looking back, Paul leaves.

Jase

I POKE MY head into Gunner's office, peering around the door. "Hey, Prez. You got a second?"

Gunner looks up from his computer screen and pushes back from his desk. "I do. Anything to get me away from looking at this fuckin' financial bullshit."

I step inside and hurry to the chair directly across from him, my movements short and jerky. I never dreamed I'd be so nervous talking to Gunner about this. He raises his eyebrows and motions for me to speak.

"I wanna open up a shop," I blurt out.

Gunner frowns. "What do you mean? You have a shop out there already."

I take a deep breath and sit up. "No. What I mean is, I want my own shop. I want to use the back bay garages to start up my own custom chopper shop."

Gunner's eyebrows creep impossibly high on his forehead. "That's a risky business, Jase."

I nod and swallow hard. "I know. Trust me, I know, but here's the thing. In the last six months, I've built three bikes by myself, and I sold them all to rich guys wanting to look badass when they're out riding." Gunner doesn't speak, but motions for me to continue. "The last chopper I sold was for more than sixty thousand."

"How did you find a buyer willing to part with that kind of cash?"

"He saw me riding it. He liked what he saw and made me an offer."

That's when I notice his apprehension fade. Now he's seeing dollar signs. "What have you done with the profits?"

"So far, I've used it to buy more tools, and I've put a big chunk of it towards building my next bike. I've already gotten three more orders for custom made choppers that I'll start after I finish the one I'm working on now. The problem is, it's just me, and I only have one of the bays. If I had all three, I could hire one or two guys to help me, and we could work on a few projects at once. More space and more hands equal more profit."

He leans back in his chair, looking thoughtful. "It sounds like a great idea, but opening a shop like that isn't a game. What happens when you get bored and decide you wanna try something else?"

My body tenses. "What do you mean, 'When I get bored?' I've been wanting to build choppers all my fucking life."

Gunner lets out a long, weary sigh. "Jase, I've known you since you were a kid. In all those years, not once have I ever seen you get serious about anything." My stomach tightens as I see where he's going with this. "I can't let you open up a business just like that, with the club's backing, so you can play Orange County Choppers. It would be a waste of money and resources."

I sit forward in my seat and look him right in the eyes. "I'm serious about this, Prez. I can make this work."

He looks at me cautiously. "I'll tell you what. You show me what you can do on your own with one more bay. If you can sell three more bikes in the next six months, we'll look at the numbers and go from there."

I feel empty—drained of purpose. I'd been nervous to pitch this idea to Gunner because I knew he'd be skeptical, but I never imagined he had such little faith in me. Never serious about anything? What the hell is that supposed to mean?

I give him a half-hearted shrug. "I'll see what I can do."

Without another word, I turn and walk out of his office. Anger washes over me. Does every motherfucker in this club think of me this way? Do they all think I'm just some screwup who can't stick to one thing?

I stalk down the hall towards the exit, my fists balled tightly at my sides. Gunner's words play back inside my head. *I've known you since you were a kid. In all those years, not once have I ever seen you get serious about anything.*

Letting out the low growl that's been building in my chest, I turn towards the wall and slam my fist right through the drywall. It doesn't make me feel better. Reaper's head pops around the corner with his eyebrows raised when he sees me yanking my arm from the fresh new hole in the wall.

"Everything cool, Jase?"

That's when I make a decision. Gunner wants me to get serious, so I'll show him how fucking serious I am. He wants me to sell three bikes? I'm gonna sell four, and I'll do it without any help from this fucking club, or it's money.

Ellen

"Bryce," I call. "Supper's ready."

I move to the fridge to pull out the milk and butter. It's been three days since Paul dropped Bryce off, and it's time my son and I have a little chat. His attitude the last couple days has been off, and I intend to get to the bottom of it.

Poking my head out the door, I look into the living room and find Bryce still sitting on the couch, playing his video game. "Bryce! It's supper time."

I can practically hear his eyes roll. "God, Mom! I'm playing a game. I'll get some later."

I don't give him another chance. Marching into the living room, I hold my finger over the power button to his PlayStation. "Now."

He scrambles up to the edge of the couch, eyes wide. "Okay, okay. Jeez." I give him the couple of seconds he needs to save his game before I press the power button. Bryce drops the controller onto the couch and walks by me, eyes narrowed in a hateful expression that I've never seen on his face before.

Following him to the table, I take my seat and spoon out some mashed potatoes onto my plate. Bryce's face is pinched and narrow as he starts plating his own food. "How was school today, Bud?"

His nostrils flare as his lips barely move. "Fine."

The hatred I feel rolling off him cuts me to the bone. I know something's going on. This isn't like Bryce. He's always such a sweet kid. "What's going on?"

"Nothing," he growls, not meeting my eyes.

"Something's obviously going on. You don't act this way, and you've never been so hateful to me. Talk to me. Tell me what's going on."

His fork lands on the table with a loud clink before he pushes back his chair and jumps to his feet. "Jesus, Mom. Nothing is wrong, other than the fact that Dad was right. You are a nosy bitch."

I don't know who's more shocked at his words, him or me. We're both frozen, eyes wide as we stare at one another. I've never hit my child, but right now, it's taking every bit of willpower I have not to slap his filthy mouth for talking to me this way. My voice is low and my eyes are hard when I say, "You need to go to your room, right now."

He doesn't argue. He quickly leaves the table and rushes off to his room, quietly closing the door behind him.

I don't know what to do. My entire body shakes with adrenaline as I try to figure out how best to deal with this.

Bryce and I have always been close. I've rarely ever had to discipline him because he tends to always be thoughtful and well-behaved. So why is he suddenly being so hateful? Well, I guess I have my answer. Paul's getting into his head by bad-mouthing me.

I take a moment to pull myself together before I get up from the table and head towards his room. I don't bother knocking before I enter.

He's sitting on his bed, his shoulders slumped. "I'm sorry, Mom."

I close my eyes and take a deep, cleansing breath. "We'll get to that in a minute. I want to know what else your father has said about me." Bryce's eyes drift off to the side, but I don't miss the fear in them. "Now, Bryce."

"He said that you baby me too much, and because of it, I'm never gonna turn into a man. He said that you're a nosy bitch that wouldn't know a good time if it jumped up and bit you in the ass." His eyes swing back to me and fill with tears. "And he said that you're an Ice Queen, and that's why you haven't managed to trap someone into marrying you."

Using the most carefully controlled tone that I can, I ask, "Do you believe those things are true, Bryce?"

His eyes widen and his head swings from side to side. "No."

I concentrate on my anger. I can't let the rage I feel towards Paul get the better of me. "Do you believe you have the right to say those things to me and call me the names your father has taught you?"

His chin quivers as he shakes his head. "No."

"I want you to collect your iPod, your PlayStation controllers, and your Wii remotes, and I want you to put them on my bed." His face falls, but he does as I ask. Taking his electronics away is like certain death to this kid. "Bryce?" I wait until he gives me his full attention. "I love you so much, but I will not tolerate you speaking to me that way. It won't happen again…are we clear?"

He nods, his jaw set and his eyes wet. "What your dad said about you wasn't very nice either." A tear slips down his cheek then. Moving closer, I wrap my boy in my arms and squeeze him tight. "He should never have said that stuff to you. And he's wrong. You're a good kid, and you're going to be a better man than any other I've ever known."

My heart breaks for my boy. Paul's going to hear from me on this. What kind of man berates a kid and his mother like that? Not any kind of man I want around my kid, that's for sure. Pulling back,

I hold him at arms length and look into his tear-filled eyes. "I'm so sorry he hurt you, Bryce."

"I'm sorry too."

Jase

IT'S BEEN THREE weeks since Gunner gave me my six-month deadline, and since then, I've been busy. I've been in this garage, working day and night to put out my best work, and it's paid off. After only three weeks, I've built an incredible custom motorcycle from scratch. Not only does she look gorgeous, but I just got back from her first test run. She drives like a fucking dream.

I step off the bike and lean her over, onto the kickstand. Stepping back, I place my hands on my hips and smile down at her. Damn, I'm good.

A low whistle sounds out from behind me. Turning, I see Reaper leaning against the door, looking at my girl. "Jesus, Jase. This is fuckin' beautiful." He steps inside and runs his fingers along the custom fender. "By far, your best work yet."

A sense of overwhelming pride fills me. I'd built bikes before, but I'd always taken my time, and only did it as a hobby. But this time, I'd thrown everything I had into this build, determined to show the rest of the club that I'm taking this seriously, and that I'm not as shallow as they think.

I pull off my helmet and grin. "Thanks, man. Have a possible buyer comin' by tomorrow afternoon to take a look."

"Fuck, that didn't take long."

I shake my head and set my helmet on the nearby tool bench. "Gonna be sad to see this baby go, though. I fuckin' love this bike."

"Then what the hell are you sellin' it for?"

I give him a pointed look. "Gunner gave me a deadline. I intend to show him, and the rest of you fuckers, that I can do this."

Reaper smirks. "Fair enough. Seems a shame to let this little beauty go to some yuppie collector."

My heart twists a little. I'd thought the same thing. The thought of my baby collecting dust in some rich guy's showcase garage makes me sick, but he's willing to pay a lot of money for this bike, and I'd be a fool to turn it down.

"It's fucking criminal, but if the crazy bastard's willing to pay me, who am I to complain?" I walk over to the light panel and start switching off the lights. "I'm in the mood to celebrate. You in?"

"What'd you have in mind?"

I flick off the final light and we step outside. "I haven't been laid in over a week, man. Let's go find some fresh pussy."

Reaper's lips twist up on one side. "I have to go check out the wiring on one of the security cameras at Chrome."

Chrome is one of several nightclubs owned and operated by the Kings. It's always packed on Friday nights, and is exactly the type of place I need to go to celebrate. "Let me grab a quick shower and hose this grease off, then we'll go."

The beat of the music thumps in my ears and vibrates the windows of the businesses surrounding the nightclub. We approach the club and walk right past the long line of people waiting to get in. The bouncer nods in greeting and steps aside.

Chrome is run by the Kings, but it's managed and cared for by Pimp, a brother known for his ruthless business sense and his well-managed crew of sexy waitresses. Aside from the bouncers, every employee in this club is female, and every one of them look sexy as hell in their tiny little uniforms, but we all know better than to touch a single one of them. Pimp may be a brother, but he protects his girls like a hellhound. You don't fuck with Pimp's ladies.

Reaper and I move straight to the raised VIP booth overlooking the entire club. The booth is always empty and available for members to use whenever they want. We each order a beer and survey the dance floor. Scantily clad women fill it, dancing with their arms raised up in the air, every one of them here for the same reason that I am, and that is to have a good time.

I watch a tall, beautiful brunette woman reach for her friend's hip. The two of them laugh and holler as they dance together, slightly offbeat from the music. I'm about to make my move when a tall preppy guy comes up behind her and kisses her neck. Taken. Fucking figures.

He takes her hand and leads her off the dance floor. I'm just about to turn away when I see the group of ladies that were hidden behind them. My heart jolts. Ellen's dancing in a tight circle with two other ladies, a wide smile spread across her face. I haven't seen her since the night at the Pig's Ear three weeks ago.

I watch her ass sway and bounce to the beat of the music, my dick hardening and pressing tightly against the zipper of my jeans. I can't take my fucking eyes off her. She looks amazing. She was fucking gorgeous in scrubs, but seeing her long legs and tight-ass in that little black skirt makes my heart skip a beat.

"Don't even think about it, man."

"Think about what?"

Reaper snorts. "Charlie asked you to stay away from that bitch. It's one woman, so pick a different one."

I cast my eyes back to the dance floor and watch as Ellen swivels her hips and laughs along with her friends. Charlie had told me to stay away from her more than once, and so far, I'd listened. But I don't wanna do that anymore. For months I've flirted with her, yet, for the most part, I've kept my distance. *Sorry, Charlie.*

"Come on, Reap. Look at those other bitches. Be a decent fuckin' wingman, would ya."

"I'm not anyone's wingman. I can find bitches all on my own."

I shrug and throw my hands up. "Your loss, brother."

Ellen

I'm so glad Julie convinced me to come out tonight. She hasn't been for a visit in months. She's only here for the weekend, but it's been so nice to have someone to talk to. Things with Bryce have calmed down over the last few weeks, but he's still not acting like himself—not by a long shot. I know something's bugging him, but he hasn't been as miserable as he was after his last visit with his father.

Paul on the other hand, has been a giant pain in my ass. He calls every day, sometimes five and six times, arguing with me and demanding to speak with Bryce. He's furious that I won't let him take him out. I won't even let him visit. After what he said to Bryce, and the way he'd grabbed my arm that day, I don't want him anywhere near either one of us.

He's threatening to take me to court and fight for full custody and even though, deep down, I know he'll never win, I'm still terrified. I know the courts would never take Bryce away from me entirely, but they may force me to allow Paul visitation rights, or possibly even give him joint custody. How could I protect Bryce from him then?

Earlier this afternoon, Bryce had been invited to a friend's house for a sleepover, and I'd been quick to say yes. Anything to make him smile again. He hasn't been defiant or nasty, but he has been sullen and moody. It worries me. He hadn't been out the door five seconds before Julie had turned to me with a wicked grin and said, "Let's go out tonight."

I tried to tell her no. I've never been to a nightclub before; I'd never had the chance. But when Julie wants something, she can be relentless. Before I knew it, she'd forced me into this short skirt and had my make-up done up heavier than I've ever done it in my life.

Now we're here, and I'm having a blast. I love to dance. I've always loved music. I may not be the best dancer, but there's something so freeing in letting go of your inhibitions and just enjoy the moment.

I'm lost in the song, my body swaying from side to side, when a pair of hands land on my waist. I look to Julie with wide eyes, hoping for some clue as to who it is, but she only looks amused. Well, she might be amused, but I'm not. You don't see strange men walking up to women in the grocery store and grinding into their ass, so why do they think it's okay to do it here?

Whipping around, I pull myself from their hold and get ready to rip them a new one, but when I see a familiar face grinning back at me, my stomach fills with a swarm of angry butterflies. God, he's beautiful. Jase should be posing for billboard ads and magazine covers.

Leaning forward, I have to shout to be heard. "What are you doing?"

I see a tiny smirk cross his face as his hands land on my hips once more, pulling me into him. "Well, I *was* dancing with you."

The butterflies go crazy and my breath catches in my throat. Placing my hands on his chest, I put some distance between his body and mine, even though I like the feel of his. "I don't think that's a good idea."

His blue eyes look at me with confusion. "Why not?"

Because you'll hurt me. I don't say it, but it's true. There's no doubt that I'm attracted to Jase. I may want him, but I can't have him. I don't want to be a notch on this beautiful man's bedpost. I respect myself more than that, and I'm not looking for casual sex.

My teeth nibble on the inside of my lip as I try to pry my eyes away from his. Finally, I find the courage to speak. "It's just not."

The stunned look on his face makes me want to take back my words. I need to get away. Without an explanation, I spin on my heel and rush towards the bathroom, praying that Julie and her friend follow. I don't need this right now. I've gone almost twelve years of playing it safe, and I'm not about to change that for anyone, not even Jase.

Sure, I've dated, but the men were always dependable, responsible, and quiet. Boring is more like it, but they were good role models for my boy. I hadn't gone out with any of them more than two or three times because they just weren't the right ones for me. I'm still holding out that someday, I'll meet a man who will be a good father to my son, and a good husband to me. Until then, I need to stay far away from guys like Jase.

I shove my way through the bathroom door and raise my hands to my flushed cheeks. God, this is silly. It was only dancing, for goodness sake.

I give myself one final look in the mirror and move to stand in the line of drunken women who are waiting to use the toilet. I use the time to calm my pounding heart and remind myself that I'm overreacting. He was flirting, which is what he's always done. Hell, he flirts with everyone.

I finish my business and wash my hands quickly before walking back through the door, intent on finding Julie.

"How do you know?"

The voice comes from behind me, and back here in the hallway, the music is quieter, so his voice bounces off the walls. I can't help it when I let out a tiny scream. "What?"

He takes a slow step closer to me, and I suddenly feel like his prey. "How do you know that it's not a good idea?"

I stare at his lips. The lower one is slightly fuller than the upper, and all I can think about is what it would feel like to take that lip between my teeth. My eyes wander from his lips to his eyes, and it's like I've been electrocuted. A jolt down my spine brings me back to the here and now.

"It was just a dance, Jase."

He steps closer, invading my space. "Exactly. It was just a dance. How is that a bad idea?"

From this distance, I can see tiny yellow flecks in the blue of his eyes. They're mesmerising. I press my back against the wall, trying to keep as much space between us as I can manage. "Jase…" I don't even know what to say without sounding like an idiot. "Look, you're a nice guy, but—"

His hand lands on the wall above my head, effectively boxing me in on one side. When he leans forward, I can barely breathe as his eyes bore into mine. "It was just a dance, El."

Does he really think I'm going to fall for this shit? I push off the wall, feeling slightly victorious when he has to back up to allow me room. "Really?"

He chuckles, but his words speak a truth that we both know. "Fuck no."

If he thinks that a sexy chuckle and a little dance is all it takes to get me into bed, he doesn't know me very well. "I'm not that girl, Jase. I've heard about you, and I'll never *be* that girl."

"Ah, so you've been asking around about me?"

"No, but I've heard enough, and what I do know is that I'm certainly not what you're looking for."

The cocky smile melts slowly from his face. "And what exactly do you think I'm looking for?"

"Not me." With that, I spin once more and march right out of the bar. Once I get outside, I text Julie and tell her I'm going to grab a cab home. I just want to get out of these tight clothes, wash away this stupid make-up, and forget that Jase Matthews even exists.

Jase

"**S**O YOU SOLD it?"

I hammer another nail into the wood and answer without looking up. "Yep. Made a fuckin' killing off it too. That guy didn't know much about bikes, but he knew he wanted that one."

Ryker hands me another board and gets to work on the other end. "Nice. I bet Gunner's impressed."

I wipe the sweat from my forehead and sit back on my heels, surveying our handiwork. We're laying the final boards to the backyard deck Charlie wanted. Ryker had started it a couple of weeks ago, but I'd been busy with my chopper. Now, with it being done, I'm ready for a cold beer and the burger he'd promised me.

"I haven't told him yet. He said three bikes, so I'll let him know once I've sold three."

The patio door slides open and Charlie steps outside with a beer in each hand. "Wow. This looks amazing, guys." She hands a beer to Ryker, then steps over a pile of tools to hand one to me. "You're almost done?"

Ryker twists the cap off the bottle and takes a long pull before answering. "I'll stain it over the weekend, but the hard part's done."

Charlie smiles wide and presses a kiss against his lips. "You did good, babe."

He reaches down to pat her ass. "Jase and I are hungry. You got those burgers ready?"

"I'll go get 'em while you fire up the grill."

She disappears inside, but is back before Ryker has completed his task. She places the plate on the table by the barbeque and turns to me. "So Ellen mentioned that she saw you at the club last night."

My chest tightens at the sound of her name. To keep from giving myself away, I wag my eyebrows and lean in closer. "You ladies were talkin' about me, were ya?"

Charlie's not amused. "We were. Ellen didn't say much, but she seemed a little upset." She lets out a heavy sigh and holds my gaze. "What are you doing, Jase? I told you she wasn't right for you."

I fold my arms across my chest and lean against the railing. "Yeah, you've told me—several times, in fact. But what you haven't told me is why. You don't think I'm good enough for your friend, Charles?"

Her expression softens a little at the use of the nickname I gave her. "Handsome, you know that's not it. It's just that Ellen has a lot of responsibility. She's got a lot going on in her life, and doesn't have time to play games with you."

"What makes you think I'm playin'?"

She continues to stare at me. I can tell her mind is racing, trying to figure out if I'm bullshitting her. "Why Ellen?"

I let my arms drop to my sides. "She's fuckin' hot, for one thing." Charlie arches her brow. "Not only that," I continue, "but she seems like a sweet girl. I got to know her a little when she was takin' care of Smoke."

I still haven't convinced her, which is clear by the look on her face. I have to get past Charlie if I have any hope of getting a shot at Ellen. "I can't fuckin' explain it. Every time I see her, she just does something to me. I don't even know why, so how the hell am I sup-posed to put it into words for you?"

"What if you can't handle her? Ellen's got some pretty heavy baggage."

"Seriously? What are you, her mother? Fuck me, Charles. I just want to see her again."

Charlie waits for me to go on, and my heart sinks. "I really like her. It's different with her." I can see the moment she caves. Her body slumps and the stubborn look on her face fades. I don't waste the opportunity. "Tell me what I have to do to see her again."

"You're relentless, you know that?" I can't contain my grin. "Fine. Ellen takes the bus to and from work. She always works the day shift, and she's working tomorrow. If you take me to work, maybe you could be outside and offer her a ride home."

Fuck. This woman is a goddamn genius. I close the distance between us and pull her into a tight hug. "You're cool as shit, Charles."

Her voice is muffled against my chest when she answers. "I know. But I swear to God, if you hurt her, I will rip your you know what right off."

"Ouch," I tease. "But that won't be necessary."

A throat being cleared behind us has me grinning even wider as I turn towards Ryker and keep Charlie in my arms. "You ladies done with gossip time, or are you gonna need another minute?"

I shrug. "I think we're done."

"Good. Now, you wanna get your fuckin' hands off my woman before I rip 'em off your body?"

I give Charlie one last squeeze and let her go. "Fuck, Ryk. When you gonna learn to share your toys?"

The punch to the arm he lands hurts like a son of a bitch, but it's worth it.

Ellen

I'm just putting the last of the groceries away when there's a loud knock on the door. If it's Paul, I don't know what I'll do. His persistent phone calls haven't stopped, and I know it's only going to get worse.

Walking to the door, I peek out the window and see a large man in a suit standing on the front step. I twist the lock and pull open the door, holding it partially closed as I peek around it. "May I help you?"

His voice is gruff and no-nonsense. "Are you Ellen McGrath?"

"Yes."

He reaches inside his pocket and pulls out a white letter envelope and thrusts it in my direction. "You've been served," he says before turning and walking down the steps to his car.

What does that even mean? I look down at the envelope, but there's no writing anywhere on it. Pushing the door closed, I turn the lock and walk back to the kitchen, tearing open the seal as I go.

Inside are four sheets of stapled papers, filled with typed words. I unfold the small stack and my heart sinks. At the top of the first page is a coat of arms, accompanied by the words, Supreme Court of Canada.

My head swims and my heart races as my eyes scan the paper, trying to make some sense of what I'm holding in my hands. I see my name and address in one column, and in the column beside it is Paul's. I feel like I can't breathe. Every breath I draw in weighs heavily on my chest as my shaking hands try to hold the paper still.

I read it over three times before I allow myself to let out the anguished sob that's been building. Paul's gotten a lawyer. In my hands, I hold a signed court affidavit, preventing me from leaving the city of Ottawa with Bryce until the court date provided at the bottom of the page—*two weeks.*

I throw down the papers and scrub my hands down my face, wiping away the tears as best I can. I need to get a handle on this. Paul has no grounds, and I'm a good mom. There's not a judge in the province that would take away a little boy from a perfectly good mother, is there?

The front door opens and in walks Bryce. "Hey, Mom."

I quickly stuff the documents back into the envelope and stow it away in the junk drawer. "Hey, Bud." I can hear a slight quiver to my voice, but pray Bryce doesn't catch it. "How was your day?"

He walks into the kitchen and heads straight for the fridge. "Fine, I guess. I'm going outside to shoot some hoops with Jimmy." He pulls out a yogurt drink and snags a granola bar from the cupboard before turning to me. His eyes narrow when as he studies me. "What's wrong?"

"Nothing," I say, my voice high-pitched and phony sounding, even to my own ears. "Nothing's wrong. Just finishing up the housework before starting supper. Go, have fun. Be a kid."

He doesn't move. Bryce has always been a smart kid, and my act doesn't fool him one bit. "You've been crying."

"Honey, I'm fine. Don't worry about your old mom."

He stares at me another minute before nodding his head and walking out of the kitchen. I don't want Bryce to know what's going on, but I don't see how at his age I can keep this from him. I need a plan. And more importantly, I need a lawyer.

Jase

CHARLIE CLIMBS OFF the back of my bike and hands me her helmet. "Thanks for the ride. Ellen should be out in a few minutes, but I don't know if she'll even go with you, you know."

"She'll come." I reply, wagging my eyebrows.

"You're terrible. Anyways, I'd wish you luck, but apparently you don't think you need it."

"I'll take whatever I can get. Have a good night, Charles."

She grins and shakes her head, turning to walk inside. I watch her go, wondering if I'm doing the right thing. Just as she reaches for the door, I call out, "Charlie?" She turns and waits. "What if she says no?"

"You're kidding, right?" she calls back.

I feel like a teenager about to go on his first date, and apparently, I sound like one too. Wanting to claim back at least a little bit of my testosterone, I simply lift my middle finger and hold it out to her, smiling wide when she laughs and walks inside. Charles is cool as hell. Ryker is one lucky bastard.

When the door closes behind her, I adjust my posture where I stand, leaning against my motorcycle, attempting to look cool and casual. I fold my arms and watch the door, then unfold them and watch it some more. Finally, I pull out my phone and play a game of Angry Birds, determined to kill some time and look more relaxed when Ellen finally walks out.

And then she does, causing my heart to race. *Jesus Christ.* What the hell is wrong with me? I have never been so nervous to see or talk to a woman before in my life. What is it about Ellen that has me tied up in so many fucking knots?

I shove the phone back in my pocket and stand straight. Ellen's walking down the walkway, digging through her giant purse for something, and hasn't even noticed me. Taking a deep breath, I decide to go for it.

"El," I call out.

Her head whips up and the shock on her face when she sees me has me smiling. "Jase? What are you doing here?"

I walk towards her. "Waiting for you to get off work. I just dropped Charlie off and she mentioned you would be leaving in a few minutes."

She goes to say something, but nothing comes out. She just stares up at me with wide, surprised eyes.

"She also mentioned that you always take the bus. I was thinking I'd give you a ride home." Her mouth closes and I see her throat move with the force of her swallow, but she still says nothing. Uncertainty fills me. Why isn't she saying anything? "So let's go."

I reach for her hand, but she pulls away. "Why?"

"Why what?"

"Why do you want to give me a ride? Why would you wait for me? I told you that I'm not interested."

I've had enough. "It's a ride home, El. Don't make it into something more."

She seems to think it over. "Fine. My back hurts, my feet are killing me, and I just want to get home. A ride with you sounds far better than an hour on a smelly city bus."

I wrinkle my nose and snort. "Flattery—I like it."

She looks at me questioningly before a giggle escapes her lips.

"Sorry, Jase. I didn't mean for that to sound so ungrateful. I would love a ride home, especially after the day I've had."

My heart leaps in my chest and I can't contain my smile. "Well, all right then." I wave my arm towards my ride. "Let's get you home."

As she passes, I slide the heavy purse off her shoulder, ready to stow it in the saddlebag. "Damn, woman. What do have in this thing?"

"I'm not a hoarder. I need everything inside that thing."

I hold up my hands in surrender. "Whoa, message received. I just hope my bike doesn't lean to the side from the weight."

I duck a half-hearted swat from her as I hand her the same helmet that Charlie had used. I start up the motorcycle and let it idle while I tighten up her helmet straps. Her brown eyes stare into mine and my stomach tightens. The vulnerability I see there makes my hands shake.

Clearing my throat, I finish with the strap and pat her on the head. "Lookin' good, El."

She rolls her eyes and motions for me to get on the bike. Grinning like a fool, I turn and swing my leg over the seat. Her hands rest on my shoulders, and I feel her body wobble a little as she gets on behind me. I can tell she hasn't done this much, if ever.

Reaching back with both hands, I grab her just under the knees and drag her body tight against mine. Raising my voice to be heard over the growl of the motor, I look over my shoulder and shout, "Point the way."

She lifts her arm and points east. I look at her, my eyes on her lips. I'd give anything to kiss those fucking lips right now, but I'm not a contortionist, and I don't exactly feel like being slapped today.

With one final look into her eyes, I smile wide and put one foot up on the foot pegs and turn, heading east.

Ellen

I haven't been on a motorcycle since I was a kid. My Uncle Mark had a Harley that he rode everywhere when the weather was nice, and there were many times he would take me with him. I'd always loved the feeling of freedom I felt when on the back of his bike.

Being on Jase's bike is different. I'm hardly aware of the ride itself. All I can focus on is the fact that my thighs are wrapped around his, and my entire body is pressed against his wide, muscular back. He smells like Irish Spring soap and laundry detergent, mixed with the surprisingly erotic scent of his leather cut.

Instead of keeping my eyes on the road, I can't take them off of the three tiny freckles on the back of his tanned neck. The urge to press my lips to that tiny trio makes my legs clench together. Praying he doesn't notice, I lean in a little closer and bring my nose just above his neck. I feel his abs contract under my hands, and know that he can feel what I'm doing, but I can't help it. His smell is intoxicating.

When his hand lands on my knee, I jump, yanked from my lust-induced sniffing. I look up and find we're approaching a red light, and it's not one I recognize. Shit. Leaning forward, I call into his ear, "We missed the turn."

His head turns and he raises a brow, an amused smirk on his face. My face heats. "We need to go back to Needham and turn left."

The light turns green and Jase nods as the bike starts to move again. As he makes the necessary turns to get us back on course, I sit behind him, silently berating myself, and feeling like an idiot. Not only does he know I was smelling him, he also knows that I was so caught up in it, I let us go almost five minutes out of the way.

Jase makes a left turn on Needham Street, which is only two blocks from my house. I point over his shoulder to show him where to pull off the road. He pulls up along the curb, right in front of my tiny bungalow.

Still feeling like a fool, I climb off and start undoing the chin-strap on my helmet. "Thanks for the ride."

He turns off the motorcycle, and the sudden silence is deafening. "You're welcome," he replies. He removes his own helmet and climbs off the bike. What is he doing?

"Relax, El. I'm just getting your bag." He pulls my purse from the saddlebag and hands it to me, looking over my shoulder. "Nice house."

I turn around and look at my home. It's not much, but it's perfect for me and Bryce, and I'm proud of it. I worked my ass off to pay for it, and in a couple of years, it will be all mine, mortgage free. The tiny brick house sits nestled between its neighbors, separated by a six-foot privacy fence along the side and back yard. There are hanging baskets on opposite sides of the small front veranda, and the majority of the front yard is taken up by the garden that I love to putter in on my days off. It's a nice, comfortable house.

I look back at him and smile. "Thanks. It's no mansion, but I'm proud of it. Being a nurse, it's what I can afford."

"Don't say it like that. Being a nurse is something you should be proud of. I watched you guys taking care of Smoke. I would never be able to do what you do."

My cheeks flush and I look down to the sidewalk, humbled by his words.

"What made you want to be a nurse?"

His question surprises me. It's personal, and probably a lot deeper than he intended for it to be. "Well, I never really wanted to be one, to be honest." I think back to when I was a little girl. I'd only ever wanted to do one thing with my life. "I always thought I'd end up becoming a doctor."

"Why didn't you?"

I shrug and smile softly, thinking of Bryce, and how much I love him. "Life happened. I don't regret it, really. I love my job. Hell, a nurse is more hands-on than a doctor. I ended up in the right place I think."

"But you still want to be a doctor," he says. It's not a question.

All I can do is shrug once more.

He moves into my space and my heart lurches before taking off on a mad race against the butterflies in my belly. He places a single finger under my chin, lifting my face so he can stare into my eyes. "You aren't dead yet, El. Anything's possible."

My mouth goes dry. Hearing his words of encouragement, something I've never heard from anyone before, makes my knees weak. His eyes lower until he's staring at my lips. It takes every ounce of willpower I possess not to lick them. His head lowers, slowly, and I know what he's about to do.

The urge to flee overwhelms me. My breathing is out of control, and I want him to kiss me so bad, but I know it's a terrible idea. A memory of the girl from the bar, slapping him across the face runs through my mind, and that pulls me out of my haze.

Pulling back, I clear my throat and hoist my purse up on my shoulder. "Thanks again for the ride."

I don't wait for a response. I run up the steps and unlock the door. I'm just about to push it open when I hear, "Same time tomorrow?"

No! Why doesn't he get that this isn't going to happen? I look over my shoulder to see him standing by his bike, a smile on his face, and his helmet in his hand. He's relentless. Shaking my head, I turn my away and walk inside.

Jase

Ellen's house is on the opposite end of the city from the club-house, and traffic is a bitch at this time of day. At this rate, it's going to take me an hour just to get back to the garage. I'm sitting at yet another stoplight in a long line of commuters in their fancy cars, when I see one that doesn't quite fit.

A large black Escalade sits about three cars behind me. It wouldn't even have caught my attention if it weren't for the loud, thumping rap music, or the heavily tattooed arms hanging out of all four of its windows.

Normally, these things wouldn't bother me, but the flash of blue I see has me on alert. Lately, we've been cautious. The Crips are a local street gang, known for wearing blue. Up until recently, we've never had much to do with them, but it seems those days are over.

Back when Ryker had met Charlie, she'd been mixed up with the Devil's Rejects MC, and not in a good way. A bunch of shit had gone down, and in the end, they'd felt the need to dole out some sort of fucked up punishment on our club. They made an attempt to take out my buddy Tease and his old lady when they were out for a ride, nearly killing them both.

After that, it was a full-on war with those sons of bitches. When we retaliated, they had been right in the middle of carrying out a deal with the Crips, and a bunch of the gang's members had gotten killed in the process. They'd fought back, even managing to get off a few shots of their own. One of them had shot me that night, taking off the tip of my ear. To make matters worse, we'd taken care of the MC, but one of the Crips had gotten away, and we've been waiting for the fallback ever since. But so far, nothing's happened. Some of the guys had mentioned seeing them around a lot lately, but this is the first time I've seen any of them since all that shit went down.

When the light turns green, I continue down the road, less relaxed than I'd been a few minutes ago. Are these fuckers following me? Coming up to an intersection, I get into the left lane, ready to make a turn. I don't need to go this way, but I wanna see if the Escalade turns with me.

Sure enough, now with only one car between us, the Escalade is right on my tail. *Fuck.* I'm still about ten minutes away from the compound, and pretty soon, I'll be in a less populated part of town. Not a place I need to be with a bunch of pissed-off Crips on my tail.

Coming to a four-way stop, I make a U-turn, looking directly at them as I drive by. A small guy in the backseat lifts his hand and makes the hand gesture of pointing a gun at me. It's a warning. I lift my middle finger and pull back on the throttle, knowing that I need to put some distance between us.

I'm just turning back onto the main road when I see the Escalade make a U-turn as well. They're coming. Driving faster than I should, I weave through traffic, intent on making it back to the compound. Surely these fuckers will disappear along the way.

I don't see them again for the rest of my ride back, and when I pull into the compound, I park my bike and jump off, ready to go straight to Gunner. Just as I'm walking across the lot, the Escalade comes up the road, slowing as it approaches. I see the passenger extend his arm, a real gun gripped tight in his hand, pointed right at me.

"Get down," I scream, alerting the people in the vicinity. I fall to my belly, sure that this is the end, but I don't take my eyes off the shooter. His eyes are cold and hard, his face twisted with hate. A single tear is tattooed under his right eye.

It plays out like a slow motion movie, no detail going unnoticed. I watch his hand move and a shot rings out, right before the Escalade guns the engine and tears off down the road. I can't move. *Am I hit?*

People start pouring out of the garage and clubhouse, everyone yelling and wanting to know what the hell is going on. Reaper comes over and helps me off the ground. "He shot at me," I say, feeling completely disconnected from my body.

I watch as people start to crowd around the front of the compound. "They didn't shoot you, Jase. For fuck's sake, man. What is it with you and always thinking you've been shot?"

"Fuck you, Reaper. That last time, I did get shot."

Reaper doesn't argue. He just shakes his head and moves to the front of the compound to see what everyone's looking at. "That's what they shot," he drawls, motioning to something up ahead.

I crane my neck and finally see what everyone else sees. Right above the entrance to our main garage and place of business, is the Kings of Korruption logo, and right in the centre of the skull is a perfectly round hole. That fucker had perfect aim.

Ellen

"Why do we even have to be here?" Bryce pouts.

Maybe I should just tell him, but how much? I had made this appointment for this evening, specifically because my neighbor, Linda, had said she could watch Bryce for me. But Linda had fallen down the stairs and twisted her ankle, resulting in a last-minute trip to the emergency room. So now I'm stuck with an appointment that I have to keep, and no way to shield my son from from the reason why.

"I have a few things to talk to the lawyer about. I won't be long. You have your iPad, so just play a game out here in the waiting room."

Bryce stares at me for a second before turning back to his game. I watch him as he plays, head bent over the tablet, noticing not for the first time, how much he looks like Paul. There is no question that he's his father's son.

Bryce shares his dad's dark hair and wide shoulders. He's taller and broader than most boys his age, and the way he narrows his eyes on the screen with a scrunched up nose is the same way I'd seen Paul looking at papers on his desk at school, or reading a text on his phone. Luckily, I see a lot of myself in him too. The smattering of freckles across his nose, his chocolate brown, heavily lashed eyes, and the tilt to his lips when he smiles are all me. Unfortunately, he also got my sharp tongue and quick wit.

"Miss McGrath?"

I look up quickly at the sound of my name to see a sharply dressed woman standing in the doorway. She doesn't seem to have a speck of make-up on her face, and her hair is pulled back into a severe bun at the back of her head. She looks over the top of her glasses at me, then to Bryce.

I stand and begin walking towards her, calling back over my shoulder. "You wait here, Bud." He doesn't reply.

I follow the severe looking woman down the hall to a door off to the right. She walks inside and indicates a chair opposite her large wooden desk for me to sit in. The room is stuffy, and smells like the old legal textbooks that line every inch of the walls.

I had chosen Stella McRae as my lawyer because she accepts legal aide, and because she could work around my work schedule. I have no idea if she's going to be good enough to keep Paul from my son, but I need to hear what she has to say.

I watch as she sits primly in her chair and pushes her glasses up on her nose. She grabs a stack of papers and taps them against her desk, then turns to me. "Miss McGrath, I have reviewed the affidavit provided by your ex-husband's attorney, and I must say, he has a strong case."

My heart sinks. "But—I haven't heard your side of the story yet," she continues. "I have a long list of questions to ask you, and then you can ask me any questions you might have. Sound good?"

I nod, my body shaking with adrenaline. Just being in this office is my worst nightmare. The fact that I have to answer this lady's questions to find out if I have a shot at keeping custody of my own son has me wanting to curl up in a ball and cry.

She picks up her pen and pulls a fresh legal sized pad of yellow paper from a drawer in her desk. "How long were you and the plaintiff married?"

"We never married," I say, my voice shaking as I try to calm my trembling body. "Paul was my boyfriend in high school for a couple of months. I got pregnant shortly after my sixteenth birthday, but Paul couldn't handle it. I never spoke to him after I had Bryce until just over a year ago, when he contacted me on Facebook."

She eyes me for a moment and sits back in her seat. She removes her glasses and places the end of one arm between her lips as she stares at me. "So you're telling me that Bryce's father has only known your son for a year?"

I nod, and my heart soars as a wolfish grin spreads across her face. "Oh, honey. Start from the beginning."

I tell her everything, and it doesn't take long. When it comes to Paul's involvement in our lives, there isn't much to tell. She asks a lot of questions, and I explain to her how my parents disowned me, and that Jackie's family had helped me out. I explain how I'd worked two jobs and gone to university to get my nursing degree while Bryce was just a toddler, and how Paul had kept Bryce out late, and how he'd grabbed my arm. I even tell her about the shitty things he's said about me to my own son, causing him unnecessary stress. She was especially interested when I told her about Bryce's behaviour since Paul came into his life.

When I finish, Stella steeples her fingers and looks off into space. I sit silently, waiting for what she has to say. With a deep breath, she leans forward on her desk. "Okay, there's good news and there's bad news. You choose which you want first."

I don't hesitate. "Bad news."

"Access. He's entitled to it." I open my mouth to protest, but she holds her hand up for me to stop. "No judge is going to deny a willing father access to his child without reasonable cause. That being said, if he's as rough and gruff as you say he is, we most definitely have a case of coercive behaviour here. I say we push for supervised visits right off the bat, and strip him of that right once we prove our case."

Makes sense. If the court is going to grant him access while we're working this out, I'd much rather it be supervised than not.

"Now the good news. Your son is old enough to have a say in this."

My eyes widen. "Bryce doesn't know anything about this."

"I'm not trying to tell you how to parent your son, Miss McGrath, but I have no doubt in my mind that he knows something's going on, especially if his behaviour has been off lately. Talk to him. Kids are intelligent and extremely perceptive. I think you might be surprised by what he has to say about all this."

I bite my lip, trying to imagine Bryce's reaction when he realizes that his father wants to take him away from me. That kind of decision seems like an awful lot to lay at the feet of a child. Damn Paul for putting us through this.

Jase

THE SUN IS shining and the birds are singing as I wait for Ellen to come out of the nursing home. It's a good fucking day. My second bike is looking sexy as hell, and I already have a couple of buyers interested in it. I haven't seen any sign of any gang members with guns following me, and I'm about to have a sexy nurse press her tits into my back for the second time. Today is my fucking day.

Ellen walks out, her hand up to shield her eyes. When she sees me leaning against my bike, she keeps walking. God, she's gorgeous. Her short blond hair is cut in a trendy style that leaves it long in the front, sweeping off to the side, and buzzed short along the sides and back.

Normally, I like my women with long hair, but when it comes to Ellen's, I don't even care. She could be fucking bald and my dick would still get hard just looking at her. Besides, the short hair draws attention to her bright eyes and high cheekbones.

I watch her approach, wondering how a woman can make scrubs look so damn sexy, when she says, "You don't give up, do you?"

A grin spreads across my face. "Not when I want something."

She laughs, handing me her purse to stow. I take it from her and widen my eyes dramatically. "What the hell? This weighs at least ten pounds more than it did yesterday. Seriously, woman, what do you have in this fuckin' thing?"

She's already fastening her own chin strap on the helmet, and doesn't bother answering me. I stow the bag and climb on, waiting until she settles her ass on the seat behind me.

"You gotta get home right away?" I ask, glancing at her over my shoulder.

"No, actually. Not today."

I start up my ride. "Good," I call back. "I'm taking you on a tour." With that, I pull back on the throttle and we head straight for the road. She wraps her arms tightly around my waist, and I revel in the feeling of her body pressed against mine.

I've had a lot of women on the back of my bike, but none of them ever had staying power. They were only there as a way to get them from wherever they were, and into my bed. Ellen is different. It feels natural having her back there, like it's her rightful place.

I keep my eyes peeled for any signs of the Crips, but there are none. Maybe after they delivered their message, they're backing off, for now. Gunner won't stand for the bullshit they pulled yesterday. We have to retaliate.

The Rockcliffe Parkway is busier than I'd expected, but it's a beautiful day. Apparently, we're not the only tourists out for a drive. We ride along in silence, the only communication being when Ellen's arm comes up and points at something worth looking at. The green trees and the crystal clear water are beautiful, and for the first time in a long time, I don't feel the pressure to entertain. I get to relax and just enjoy her company.

We motor down the road, passing trees, lakes, and fields of corn. The simplicity of it all is something I feel like I've needed. I mean, when was the last time I'd just gone for a ride to clear my head? Far too long.

After about forty minutes on the road, Ellen leans forward to call into my ear, "I need to get home now."

I do what I need to do to get the bike moving in the right direction. Twenty minutes later, we're pulling up to her front door. Ellen slides off the bike, looking slightly bow legged.

I point down to her thighs. "You need to ride more."

"I really do. God, that was exactly what I needed. Things have been kind of crazy for me lately, and I didn't know just how much I needed to escape for a little while.

"Crazy how? Charlie mentioned the other day that you were going through some stuff."

Ellen presses her lips together and shakes her head before reaching to undo the chin strap on her helmet. "Don't you worry about it. Just know that I really enjoyed myself."

Sliding off the bike, I take a step towards her. "Don't do that. Don't blow me off." Reaching out, I hook my finger under the chin strap and use it to pull her face to mine, my lips mere inches from hers. "In case you haven't noticed, I want to be around you. I want to know all about you, El. But I can't do that if you keep pushing me away."

"Mom? What's going on?"

Our heads whip to the side, and standing in front of us is one pissed-off looking kid. I can tell just by looking at him that he's Ellen's. He has her eyes.

"Bryce! What are you doing home? I thought that you were—"

"Jimmy had a doctor's appointment." He waves a hand in my direction. "Who's this guy?"

I watch as Ellen stands there, mouth hanging open in shock, so I take a step forward and stick out my hand. "Hey, man. I'm Jase, a friend of your mom's."

The kid's eyes narrow on my outstretched hand longer than necessary before wrinkling his nose at me in disgust and storming back inside the house.

Ellen's hand flies up to cover her mouth. "Shit. I'm sorry, Jase. I gotta go." Whipping the helmet off, she thrusts it into my arms and runs after her son.

All I can do is stare after her, one thought running through my head.

Ellen has a fucking kid?

Ellen

"Bryce, we need to talk," I call through his closed bedroom door. The response I get is the sound of his music being cranked up even louder to drown out the sound of my voice. I twist the doorknob and find that it's locked.

Using the heel of my hand, I pound on the door loudly. "Bryce Alexander! You open up this door or I will take it off its hinges!"

Down the hall, the phone rings, distracting me from screaming at my kid. Worried that it might be work, I hurry into the living room and scoop up the receiver from where it lays abandoned on the couch. It's Julie.

"Hello?"

"Hey, girl. How's it going?"

"Not so good at the moment."

Julie's voice rises. "What? Why not? And what is that awful noise? It sounds like you're at a concert, for God's sake."

I sigh and move out onto the front step so I can hear myself think. "No concert. Just Bryce throwing a tantrum."

"Bryce?" she says, surprise dripping from her voice. "My Bryce? I don't believe it. What's he so upset about."

I sigh again, this time heavier. "Yes, your Bryce. He's not the angel you think he is, you know. Anyways, he was supposed to be at his friends after school until suppertime, so I went—" Crap. I don't know how much to tell her. I hadn't mentioned my recent encounters with Jase.

"Spill it, girl," she says, suddenly all business.

"Fine. I went for a ride with Jase on his motorcycle." Julie's loud squeal pierces my ear. "When he dropped me off today, we were talking out on the sidewalk. I think he was about to kiss me, but Bryce walked out, and he was *not* happy."

"Who cares what Bryce thinks? Has he even met Jase?"

"No," I reply, "but that's not the point. The point is, Bryce obviously isn't ready to see me with a man."

"Oh please," she scoffs. "Look, I love Bryce like he's my own. You know that. But Bryce isn't ever going to be ready to see you with a man because he's never *seen* you with a man. He needs to get over it and learn to share his mommy. It's different if he doesn't like him because the guy's an asshole or something, but to not like him simply because you do? Well, that's just selfish."

I chew my lip. She's right. It's not that I've never dated since Bryce was born, it's more that I'd never let Bryce see me dating or meet my dates. I have no intentions of introducing him to someone until I know we're serious. And so far, that hasn't happened.

"Look, Ellen. You're a strong, successful woman. Not only that, but you're gorgeous. Any man that meets you is going to want you. But Jase isn't just any man. I saw the way he looked at you that night in the bar. He likes you."

I roll my eyes. "Of course he likes me. We're friends."

"No, I mean he *likes* you, likes you. That man has no interest in being just friends. Let me ask you a question."

"Okay."

"Do you like him?"

"Of course I like him. He's funny, he's gorgeous, and he smiles all the time. But he's also a slut. I don't like that part about him. I have a son to raise, Julie. I don't want to get caught up in biker whore drama and regular STD exams."

Julie laughs. "Biker whore drama?"

"I'm serious, Julie! The club has women that hang around at the clubhouse, without any panties, waiting to "service" the guys. It's disgusting. Not only that, but they get all territorial if someone like me comes around. Charlie and my friend Laynie have had their share of biker whore drama. It's a real thing."

"Whatever." She chuckles. "You need to do what makes you happy, Ellen. And if that means hooking up with Jase on occasion, so be it. If that means a serious relationship with a sexy man whose eyes scream "fuck me," that's even better. Either way, Bryce doesn't need to know the dirty details, and he doesn't get a say. He's your kid. You're his parent. Besides, Bryce isn't going to be around forever, you know. In about seven years, he's going to go off to college, meet some chick, and only be back for Thanksgiving and Christmas. By then, your tits will be saggy and your pubes will be grey. It'll be too late to find a man then. You willing to take that risk?"

"My pubes will not be grey in seven years. Besides, I'll shave them off if they do."

"Whatever. Give that poor muscled biker a chance, okay? And who knows, maybe he can take care of your little Paul problem. Make him swim with the fishes."

"I think that's what gangsters say, Jules, not bikers."

"You get the picture."

I can't help but laugh. "You're an ass."

Eight

Jase

I'M LEANING OVER the partially built motor in the garage, wondering how the fuck I didn't know that Ellen had a kid, when Gunner walks in. He stands in the doorway and looks around at the mess of parts lying all over the floor. I put down my wrench and grab a rag, standing up as I attempt to wipe some of the grease from my fingers.

I motion to the floor. "It doesn't look like much, but it won't take long to have this baby up and runnin'."

He nods and takes a step inside. "Looks like you've come a long way in just a couple of days. Didn't you just start this one?"

I look over at him, surprised. I haven't been keeping Gunner up to speed on my work out here, intending to tell him when my quota was met so he could see how hard I've been working. "Yeah, but I finally got the rest of the parts in yesterday. It'll go fairly quick if all goes according to plan."

Gunner walks over to the motor and checks out the different parts, kneeling low to get a better look. His finger runs along one of the cylinder heads. "She's gonna be a fast one," he declares.

"I'm countin' on it."

He stands and heads over to the work bench where he leans his large frame against it. Gunner is a big man, and his presence in the room, though welcome, is still commanding. "Reaper told me you sold your first bike."

I toss the rag on the pile in the corner. "Looks like Reaper doesn't know when to mind his own business."

Gunner chuckles. "He told me because he thinks I'm being a dick about all this. He's proud of you, and wanted me to know."

"He said that?" I ask in disbelief.

"Fuck no. He just told me that you already sold a bike, and that it was pretty fuckin' amazing. Said you would've kept it for yourself, but were tryin' to prove somethin' to me. Told me I was too hard on you."

"We are talking about Reaper here, right? Big, hairy fucker, with hands the size of dinner plates?" I can't imagine that grumpy bastard saying any of that in my defense.

"Yeah. Fucked with my head too."

I don't say anything. What is there to say?

"Look, Jase. I want you to know that I think you're an incredible mechanic. I've seen your work, and it's always the best. I'm proud of you too." My chest gets tight as I stare back at him. "I know your old man didn't have much to do with raising you, and you had to figure out a lot of shit on your own. I watched you grow up, and I know it wasn't easy for you. I just wanted you to know that I see you workin' your ass off out here, and I see how hard you're tryin' to prove me wrong. Keep it up."

I blink. "I plan on it."

He grins. "I know you do. And I'm countin' on you to prove my ass wrong."

His phone rings. He pulls it from his pocket and grumbles down at the number before tapping the screen. "Yeah?" I watch as his expression goes from annoyed to alert, then settles on cold and angry. With his brows drawn low, he barks into the phone, "When?"

His jaw ticks as he listens to the caller. "Get them back here. I'll call Reaper."

With that, he shoves the phone back in his pocket and stalks towards the door. Just as he's about to leave, he turns to me. "Need you at the clubhouse in fifteen minutes. Send out a text and let the others know, and tell them it's an emergency." He jams his fingers through his hair. "Fuck," he shouts. "I was supposed to go to my daughter's tonight. She's gonna fuckin' kill me. It was a big deal for her."

"Sorry, Prez." I murmer, not sure what's going on. He waves me off and stalks across the parking lot to the clubhouse. I activate my phone and send out a group text to every brother, telling them to get their asses back to base.

Ellen

I'm at work, enjoying my lunch in the break room when my phone rings. It's an unknown number. I hesitate, wondering if I should answer it, or let it go straight to voicemail. Even with the impending court date tomorrow, I still have to screen my calls at all hours of the day.

Paul won't stop. I never answer his calls, but he leaves messages for Bryce, as if Bryce is hearing the messages himself. They're long, and unbelievably creepy.

The one instance, I did make the mistake of answering. Paul had gotten very gruff and confrontational, demanding that I let him speak with his son. I'd hung up, right after he'd threatened to show up at my house and shove my phone up my ass. I keep the phone calls listed on my phone, ready to show the judge exactly what I've been dealing with, but I wish there was a way to go back and record that particular conversation.

Worried that it might be important, I answer. "Hello?"

"Hey, El."

His voice is smooth as silk, and makes my heart race. "Jase?"

"Yeah. Charlie gave me your number."

I don't know what to say. My heart is firmly lodged in my throat, and the butterflies in my belly are threatening to carry me away. I didn't think I'd even hear from Jase again once he learned I had a kid, and after the way Bryce had spoken to him, I figured he'd be long gone by now.

"I just wanted to call and let you know that I wouldn't be able to pick you up from work today. Something came up here at the clubhouse, and it's gonna keep me tied up for a while."

I clear my throat and try to control the quiver in my voice. "You were supposed to pick me up?"

"El."

He says it just like that, like I should know better. "I didn't know if I would hear from you again after yesterday," I admit.

"Please," he snorts. "It takes more than a pissed-off kid to scare me away. In case you haven't noticed, I'm kind of a badass."

I can't help the laugh that escapes my lips. "Really? I hadn't noticed at all."

"Nah, you noticed. And you liked it."

"Okay. So you're not picking me up. I appreciate you letting me know."

"I want to see you. I can pick you up tomorrow."

"I'm not working tomorrow."

"Well then, let's go for a ride."

I bite my lip to hide my smile, my heart thumping at the excitement I hear in his voice. He really does want to see me again, and that's good for any girl's ego, but it's especially good for mine.

"I can't," I say, surprised at how disappointed it makes me feel. "I have plans tomorrow."

"Hot date?" he teases. If he only knew how badly I wished that were true. I would much rather be on a date with Jase than sitting in a stuffy old courtroom with Paul and his vulture of a lawyer.

"Yep. Sorry."

"The next day then," he says, clearly not giving up.

I can't contain my smile. "I can do the next day. I'm off that day too."

"I'll pick you up at eleven. We'll grab some lunch."

"Okay," I whisper. God, I hope I don't end up regretting this, but Julie's right. I need to live my life too.

"Okay," he says. "See you then."

"See you then."

"Oh, and El?"

"Yeah?"

"Pack a swimsuit."

I hear his soft chuckle just before the phone disconnects. I can't believe I just said yes. I just accepted a date with Jase Matthews.

Jase

AS SOON AS I hang up the phone, I hurry across the lot and into the clubhouse. Everyone else is starting to arrive, but there's no sign of Gunner. Bosco comes in and looks around the room, stopping when his eyes land on me. His long legs eat up the distance between us.

"What's going on? Prez doesn't usually hold church at this time of day."

"Don't know. He got a call that pissed him off, told me to get everyone here for church, but I haven't seen him since."

Ryker comes rushing in, Reaper hot on his heels, medical bag in hand. This isn't good.

The two men hurry down the hall without a glance in our direction, moving towards the bedrooms in the back.

I look around. Just about everyone is here. The Kings of Korruption is changing. Not long ago, we were down to only ten patched members. We'd done some recruiting since then, and now we've become a larger group with over twenty patched members, both young and old. Everyone has a job to do, and everyone knows their place. Seeing Lucy and Pepper over in the corner, I realize that even the whores have shown up to see what's going on.

By the time Tease arrives, we've already been sitting here for twenty minutes, but there's been no movement from down the hall. We wait another fifteen before he stalks over to the bar. "Fuck this, man. I need a fuckin' beer."

He's pulling one from the fridge when Ryker comes down the hall and into the room. "Church in five, boys." His voice sounds drained and weary. I catch his eye and raise my brow, wanting to know what the hell is happening down there, but he shakes his head.

Five minutes later, everyone is in their seats around the table, or along the side walls. Nobody says anything as we walk inside. I see two of our older members, Slots and Shady, sitting in their places, their faces beat to hell. Shady has his arm in a cast.

"Let's get to it, shall we?" Gunner drawls. "As you can all see, Slots and Shady had a little trouble today. The two of them were out on a supply run and stopped at a gas station, but never bothered to notice the crew of Crips that had probably been following them the entire fucking ride."

I watch the faces of every man in the room, and they are pissed. These fucking Crips. They seem to get bolder every day.

"Believe it or not, these two were lucky. It could've been a whole lot worse. I'd have them tell you the story, but it seems Slots' jaw is broken, and he needs to get his ass to the hospital so they can wire the fuckin' thing shut, so I'll summarize. They stopped at the gas station over on Hillside, went inside to pay, and when they came out, their bikes were gone. There were five gangbangers waiting to drag them around back and kick their asses, and as you can see, they did."

Slots and Shady look up from the table while Gunner speaks, and I feel my anger boiling close to the surface. Neither one of them are big fighters, both of them tough in their own way, but not known for cracking skulls. The fact that it took a group of them to beat the shit out of two old men is a joke.

"Those Crips could have killed these two, but they didn't," Gunner continues. "They didn't because they weren't looking for a war...yet." I snap my eyes to Gunner and I'm pretty sure the other guys do to. "This was a warning. Those fuckers know we killed their men, and they aren't going to let it go. They're biding their time, but make no mistake. They're coming for us."

Ryker and I exchange a look. He's thinking what I'm thinking. The last time something like this happened, our prospect, Mouse, got shot and killed, gutting every single brother in here. We can't let that shit happen again.

"We're back to vigilance boys. You know the drill. No man alone, always carry a gun, and keep your eyes peeled for suspicious vehicles carrying gangbangers. Any questions?"

Reaper speaks first, "Aren't we gonna fuckin' do something about this? Retribution? We can't just let this shit slide."

Gunner nods. "Oh, we're not. I put a call into Tip, my contact with the Bloods. Told him we need some more intel on where these fuckers hang out, where they live. He's gathering the info for me now, and I should have it by the end of the day. After that, we'll figure out a plan of attack, but trust me when I say that this will not go unpunished. Nobody fucks with the Kings of Korruption." He looks around at all of us, his eyes fierce and angry. "Anything else?"

Nobody says a word. Gunner lifts his gavel and brings it down with a bang. "Then we're done here. Go home, fuck your women, and for the love of God, watch your backs."

Ellen

A brief phone call last night with Stella McRae did nothing to mentally prepare me for the fear I I felt when I walked into this courthouse this morning. My heart hammers against my chest and my mouth runs dry when I enter the crowded waiting room. Stella had told me that only her and Paul's lawyer would go inside the courtroom to present our cases to the judge. I haven't seen her yet, but I can only assume she's here somewhere, and is much more prepared for this than I am.

Long wooden benches line all four walls, each crammed full of people doing their damnedest to ignore everyone else. I find an empty space between a young girl in her early twenties who looks bored out of her mind, and a tall, attractive, dark-skinned man in his thirties. Neither acknowledges me when I sit.

Looking around, I'm relieved to see that Paul isn't here. *Maybe he won't show. Maybe he was all talk.* I barely finish that thought before he struts into the room, his shoulders squared, and his eyes narrow in on me.

He walks over and stands in front of me, smirking. "Ellen."

I look up at him, not knowing how to respond. My lawyer told me that under no circumstances was I to engage Paul in any conversation whatsoever. She told me that I should avoid him at all costs and document everything he says when he attempts to contact me.

"Oh, what? Now you're just going to ignore me?"

Before I can respond, Stella walks in alongside a man, both in black robes. They stop and she motions for me, while the man next to her motions for Paul.

Walking off to the side where we can speak privately, Stella keeps her voice low. "I'll go in there, plead your case, and hear what the plaintiff's party has to say. There's no doubt in my mind that the judge will remand this case to a later date. He's going to want clarification and evidence on some of the issues being brought forth. You just have to wait out here and be available in case the judge wants to talk to you, but I doubt he will."

"Okay," I respond, my body wound tight with fear. Stella turns and heads for the door, waiting for the bailiff to open it. Just as she's about to go in, she gives me a wink and disappears inside.

Paul's lawyer must have spoken to him about talking to me because he takes a seat on the far side of the room. Though he doesn't attempt to converse with me again, he stares at me the entire time, making me squirm in my seat. The man to my left leans over and raises his chin in Paul's direction.

"That your ex?"

I give him a tired smile and answer, "Yes."

"Guy's a creep. Good on ya for gettin' away from that crazy fucker."

I smile wide. "How can you tell he's creepy?" I whisper back.

"Look at the way he's lookin' at ya. That shit's not cool." He doesn't take his eyes off Paul as he speaks. "When you leave, let me walk you to your car, okay?"

I pull away in surprise. "How do I know you're any safer?"

He looks away from Paul and grins at me. "I guess you don't, but I will tell ya that I'm a happily married man." He points at his wedding ring. "And I'm worried that this guy will give ya trouble when you try to leave. You don't need that."

Warmth fills my belly at his kindness. His wife is one lucky lady. "Okay, but I don't have a car. I'm calling a cab."

"Then I'll wait with ya for your cab." I can tell he's not going to budge on the issue.

"Thank you," I whisper.

Just then, the doors to the courtroom creak open and both lawyers walk into the room. Stella motions for me to follow her, her mouth drawn into a tight line. I follow her up a steep set of concrete stairs and down a narrow carpeted hallway, right into a small interview room.

I take a seat next to her and wait for her to speak. "That Paul is a real piece of work, and he's not going to go down without a fight. This is what we have. If you agree, you sign this paper and we can all go home until the next court date, which will be in two weeks."

She holds a stack of papers out to me, but uses her finger to point at each paragraph as it explains the terms. "The judge has granted Paul weekly visitation, but since he's had limited contact with Bryce, she agreed that supervised visits are best while we continue our case." Her finger moves to the next paragraph. "Paul claims that you moved out of your parents' house in an attempt to hide from him when your child was born."

I blink at her in complete shock. "My parents kicked me out, and I was a child myself. I went to live with my friend and her family, and Paul and I continued to go to the same school for the rest of that year. I never hid from him!" My nostrils flare and I can feel the heat of my rage right to the tips of my ears.

"Do you have someone to prove that?"

I don't hesitate. "School records? My best friend has been with me through it all, so she can testify to all of it."

"Good. Now, the last thing that was brought up is that you are heavily involved with a well known organized crime ring."

My mouth drops to the floor. "What? I'm a nurse. I take care of dying people."

"According to Paul, your son contacted him yesterday, scared because you were affiliated with the Kings of Korruption motorcycle club. Is this true?"

I can't breathe. Bryce had called Paul about Jase? Was Bryce scared of Jase? And an organized crime ring? I know the Kings have a reputation, but is that what they are? "I have a friend I work with who's married to one of their members. I know some of the guys because their friend was in my care, but I don't know anything about organized crime. They're just a bunch of guys that ride motorcycles as far as I'm concerned."

Stella's lips press into a thin, harsh line. "I'm afraid the judge doesn't see it that way. The Kings are known for their illegal activity, and if you're affiliated with them in any way, you make Paul's case much stronger."

Bile begins to rise up my throat. I listen to the rest of Stella's rundown, desperately trying to understand everything she says, but all I can think of is that even being friends with Jase could cost me my son. I haven't even left the courthouse yet when I send him a text to cancel our date.

Me: I'm sorry, Jase, but no date tomorrow. And no more rides home. I need to focus on my kid.

Jase

IT'S ELEVEN O'CLOCK the next day when I pull up in front of Ellen's house. I'd gotten her sorry excuse for cancelling our date, and it seems like her and I need to have a little chat about that. We'd made plans, and I have every intention to follow through on them.

Walking up the steps to her house, I realize just how quiet her neighborhood is. The perfect neighborhood for a family. It's certainly not the type of place I've ever spent any amount of time in— I'd never lived in a house before in my life. My dad and I had a shitty apartment once, but for the most part, we lived at the clubhouse. It made it easier for my dad to do club shit and get laid.

I raise my fist and knock on the door. Hearing her footsteps coming closer from inside, I prepare myself for an argument. If there's one thing I've learned about Ellen in the last couple of weeks, it's that she's consistent. She's into me, I know she is, but she won't let herself admit it.

The door swings open and Ellen quickly grabs my arm, yanking me inside. I'd expected her to throw a fit while I was still outside, so already, I feel like I've won.

"What are you doing here?" she hisses. "Didn't you get my

text?"

I cross my arms and stare at her. "I got it. I just didn't like it."

"Well too bad!" she cries. "Whether you liked it or not, I meant it. No dates, no rides, no nothing—God! Why are you so fucking stubborn?"

Dropping my arms to my sides, I take three steps towards her, crowding her personal space so she has no other choice but to look at me. "Take a look in the mirror, El, 'cause you give me a run for my money in that department, and watch your tone. I don't disrespect you, and I expect the same courtesy."

Throwing her arms up in the air, she lets out an angry growl. "You don't get it. Look, I need you to go, right now. Hop on your motorcycle and just *leave*."

"What am I not understanding here?" I don't get why she's so angry, but I don't like the way she's talking to me. "I thought we were supposed to go for a fuckin' ride this afternoon. Then I get some bullshit text blowing me off, yet again. Well, you know what? Forget it. I can take a hint." I turn to leave, my whole body tense with anger, and my head screaming that this is wrong. Just as I'm about to walk out the door, I turn back and give her a withering look. "I get it. You're an independent woman and all that shit, but sweetheart, you're gonna be a lonely woman if you continue to keep all your shit to yourself. You need to find someone to rely on and help you work through it, 'cause I'm done." Turning back to the door, I put my hand on the doorknob.

"God!" she screams. I turn back around, shocked at her outburst. "I'm losing my mind, okay? I have some pretty heavy shit going on right now, and I need to focus on that. I was really looking forward to going out with you today, but my lawyer told me that Bryce had called his father and told him that you were here. The judge didn't like it, so I can't see you anymore. If I do, I could lose my kid."

"Okay." I take a step closer. "Can we try that again, but slower this time?"

Ellen slaps her palm against her forehead and lets out a frustrated groan. "My son's father is taking me to court for custody of my son." I nod, indicating for her to go on. "We had our first court date yesterday, and apparently Bryce—my son—called his father after you left the other day. He told him that you were here with me, and that you were a member of the Kings."

I frown. "How the hell did he know that?"

Ellen rolls her eyes. "He's a kid, Jase, not an idiot. Your vesty thing gave it away."

"Vesty thing?" I point at my leather. "You mean my cut?"

"Whatever," she exclaims. "Anyways, Paul brought it up in court as a way to get my son from me, and my lawyer told me that if I had anything to do with you, or anyone from the Kings, that Paul could win." She leans in and stage whispers, "She said you're involved in organized crime."

I blow out a heavy breath, trying to wrap my head around everything she's told me. "Who is this Paul guy anyways?"

"He was a guy I dated back in high school. He was a football player, he was popular, and he ran like hell when I got pregnant at sixteen. I didn't hear from him, not once, until just last year. He looked me up on Facebook."

I frown. "Why is he trying for custody after all these years?"

She folds her arms across her chest, almost as if she's trying to protect herself. I don't like it. "He doesn't like my rules. He wants to take Bryce away from me entirely." I grit my teeth. What kind of man takes a boy away from his mother? "He's a bully, trying to put me in my place. And after yesterday, I think he might get the chance to do just that."

Without ever having met him, I know exactly what kind of man he is. He's one of those guys who couldn't lose in high school. They got by, bullying those that were weaker than them, and scraping by in class because their coach needed them on the team. They got lots of tail and scored a few touchdowns. After they graduated, and all that went away, it left them bitter and angry. They became people who strong-arm others into doing what they want to feel powerful again, just like they did in high school. I hate fuckers like that.

I ask the one question I need to know the answer to before I say anything else. "Has he ever hurt you or the kid?"

She shakes her head sadly. "No. He grabbed my arm the last time

64

he was here, but he left right after, and I haven't let him see Bryce since."

"Did he hurt you?" I growl.

"I'm tough," she whispers, her brown eyes boring into mine.

"You want me to deal with this guy?"

"What? God, Jase, no! Why would you say that? I don't want him dead!"

I can't help but laugh at the mortified look on her face. "Babe, relax. I wasn't talkin' about offing the guy. I meant have a little chat, man to man." I turn my head and give her a questioning look. "What kind of guy do you think I am?"

She blows out a breath and giggles. "Sorry. I don't even know what I'm saying. I feel like my entire world is just spinning out of control, and I don't know what to think about anything. But no, I don't need you to talk to Paul. It's sweet of you to offer, but he would just use that against me. I have no doubt. The only way to make this better is to stop seeing you."

I don't miss the sad look in her eyes when she says it. "Are you sure about that, El? 'Cause I don't like that idea at all."

"I'm sure. Bryce is everything to me, Jase. I have to do whatever it takes to make sure I don't lose him."

My gut clenches at her words. "You're a good mom, El." I lean in and kiss along her cheek. "Bryce is a lucky kid."

She lifts her hand to her chest, her eyes shiny with tears as I walk towards the door. I pull it open and turn back to her. "If you ever need someone to unload on, give me a call. You don't need to do this all by yourself." I know that I need to go and give her the chance to keep her family intact, so with those final words, I turn and walk out of Ellen's life.

Ellen

Watching Jase walk out the door is harder than I thought it would be. We haven't spent a lot of time together, and there's a lot we don't know about the other, but deep down, a part of me had wanted all that to change. It's the part of me that stands frozen, staring at the door, and listening to the sound of his motorcycle roaring down the street and out of my life, once and for all.

"In case you can't tell, I want to be around you. I want to know all about you, El. But I can't do that if you keep pushing me away." God, Jase.

I swallow down the giant lump in my throat. The other part of me, the part that was afraid to get attached to Jase, only to wind up with a broken heart, breathes a sigh of relief. Imagine how hard that would have been if we had been closer; if we had gotten to know each other better. I lean my forehead against the wall and squeeze my eyes closed. It's better that we sever all ties now.

A knock on the door breaks me from my thoughts. I rush to answer it, assuming it's Jase, back to convince me to change my mind, but it's not.

"Paul? You can't be here."

He chuckles without a trace of humour. "Shut up and listen. This court shit is going to get messy, and it's costing me a fucking fortune. My lawyer's told me that I have a really good shot at beating you, but I doubt you want that. So, I'm here to make a deal."

I can't believe this asshole. "Are you kidding me right now? No, I will not make a deal with you. This is my son we're talking about, not some used car, or an old lawnmower that we can just agree to share." I step back inside and close the door enough that I'm peeking around it at him. "You need to leave, Paul. Let our lawyers do the talking from now on."

I go to slam the door shut, but he stops it with his foot. My heart races as he uses his entire body to shove it open again.

"You're making a big mistake, Ellen. A huge mistake. I want you to know that when I win custody of Bryce, it'll be a cold day in Hell before you ever see him again."

"Just get out!" I scream, trying to shove the door closed, even with his body in the way. It's all I can do to keep the angry tears from spilling over. "Go, you son of a bitch, or I'm calling the police."

He gives me an evil smile and puts his hands up, backing out of the door. "I'll go, but only because tomorrow is my first supervised visit with Bryce, and there's not one thing you can do to fuck that up. See you in court, bitch."

I watch in shock as he turns on his heels and walks casually to his car. Just as he's about to get in, he turns, giving me a cocky salute. Once I see that he's gone, I close the door, making sure it's locked tight. My entire body shakes as I crumple to the floor when the tears I'd been holding start to fall.

This is too much. I can't handle this. Losing Jase before I even had him, the fear of losing my son in this terrifying, impersonal court case, and the fear of Paul in general, threaten to consume me. I don't know how to stop this. I don't know what to do.

I pull my knees up to my chest, circling them with my arms, and I cry. I let all the sadness and anger out in one long crying session. So many tears fall, I feel like Alice in Wonderland, about to be washed away in a sea of salty sadness.

Gradually my tears subside. *Enough crying, Ellen. It's time to man up, girl, and this isn't helping.*

Standing from my place on the floor, I check myself over in the hallway mirror. I look a mess. My eyes are red and puffy, tear stains running down my cheeks. I can't cry pretty like those girls you see on TV. No, not me. I cry ugly, fat tears, complete with dripping nose and red splotchy face. I am the ugliest crier I know.

I go to the bathroom and try to fix myself up a bit. Bryce will be home soon, and I don't want him to know I've been crying. I need to talk to him, especially now that he'll be going to a family centre for supervised visitation with his father.

I've never felt so alone; not even when my family disowned me. Thank God for Julie and her parents. Jase is right. I need to have someone to talk to about this, or I'm going to lose my mind, but who? Nobody would understand. They'd sympathize, sure, but would anybody really get what I'm going through?

I blow out a long breath and look around my house. I'm going to have to get through this on my own. I can do this, because I have no choice.

Jase

"COME ON, MAN. You can't tell me you don't see the irony."

I roll my eyes and toss my beer cap at Ryker's head. "Fuck you, asshole. This shit isn't funny."

He smirks and shakes his head, leaning forward to pick at the label on his beer bottle. "You're right, it's not. You've been fuckin' bitches left and right, without ever looking back. Now you've finally found one that you want, and she's not interested."

"She's interested," I drawl, wagging my eyebrows. "She just has all that shit going on with her ex. Man, the guy sounds like he needs his ass kicked."

Ryker nods. "He does, so let's do it. Let's find this asshole and set him straight."

I crack my knuckles and curl my lip. "Oh, trust me. I intend to. Just need to find out who the fuck he is first."

A commotion from the entrance of the clubhouse draws our attention. Gabby, Gunner's daughter, is standing by the door, talking to two of our members with her arms flailing, looking worried. The two guys look to us, concern heavy in their expressions.

Abandoning our beers, we stand as one and move in Gabby's direction. "What's going on, sweetheart?" Ryker asks.

"My dad," she says, clearly trying to control her emotions. "I can't get a hold of my dad."

"Okay," Ryker says in a soothing voice. "Let's get you sitting down. Your father's a busy man, Gab. He's probably not able to answer the phone right now. Nothin' to worry about."

"No!" she exclaims, yanking away from Ryker. "You don't understand. He was supposed to be at my place two hours ago. He was going to come over and fix the dishwasher, and said he had something to tell me. He never showed, and he never called. That's not right. Since we started talking again, he's been really good about making sure I know he's not standing me up. Something's wrong."

Ryker and I exchange a look.

She's right, something's off. Since reconnecting with his kids a couple months ago, I've seen Gunner interrupt church meetings to call Gabby and let her know he was gonna be late for something they had planned. He loves his kids, and knew that with their history, they still feared he'd leave them again.

Ryker pulls his phone from his pocket and taps the screen a few times before pressing it to his ear. I can faintly hear the ringing coming from the other end of his call. He doesn't take his eyes off me, and I don't miss the fear hiding there.

He taps the screen again a couple more times and puts it to his ear. More ringing, still no answer.

I hear Tess's voice on the other end, instructing the caller to leave a message. Tess is Gunner's old lady, and for her not to answer the phone is just strange. The woman has that thing in her hand twenty-four seven.

Ryker disconnects and taps the screen a third time. Putting it to his ear, I hear it ring twice before it's picked up. "Bosco, I need you to do me a favor. Who you with?"

I stare at Ryker, waiting to hear what the hell is going on. His forehead creases. "Shank? Who the hell is Shank?"

I can't help but chuckle. Ryker never was good with names. Shank is our newest prospect, only coming on board a few weeks ago. He's a huge son of a bitch, but I don't know much about him other than that.

"Whatever," Ryker continues. "Take him with you. I need the two of you to run over to Gunner's house and see if him or Tess are there. If you see him, tell him that Gabby is looking for him, and so am I."

Ryker jams his phone back in his pocket and takes Gabby's hand. "Come on, sweetheart. Let's get you a beer. Those guys aren't too far from your dad's house."

Moving to the bar, I snag a beer and twist off the cap, handing it to Gabby.

She takes it from me and gives me a nod before tipping the bottle back and swallowing down half of it in one go. It's not hard to tell she's Gunner's daughter.

Gabby sets the bottle down heavily on the table. "I'm worried," she whispers.

Ryker doesn't say anything. He looks worried too. I move in and take her hand. "I know, Gab, but we're gonna find him, okay? Let's find something else to talk about." I look around the room, desperate to find anything to distract us from the wait.

"Laynie tells me you're finally seeing that Ellen woman," Gabby says.

"Yeah, I was, but she broke it off."

Gabby's eyes widen and her mouth drops open. "What? Why?"

I give her the short version, without telling her too much of Ellen's story. That's not mine to share. I'm just finishing up when Ryker's phone rings.

"Yeah?" he barks.

I don't hear what's said, but Ryker's expression says it all. "Okay, hold tight," he chokes out, his voice choked up with emotion. He disconnects the call and his gaze shifts to Gabby. "Bosco found him. He's dead, Gabby. Him and Tess."

"No," she cries. "No!"

"I'm so sorry, sweetheart," he whispers before stalking out to his bike and leaving me with a woman who just learned she'd lost her father.

Ellen

Bryce is crawling into bed when I walk into his room. "Hey, Bud. Can we talk for a sec?"

He arranges the blankets across his lap and shrugs. "Sure."

I sit down on the edge of his bed, trying to figure out exactly what I should say. Nothing can prepare you for having to tell your son that his father is trying to get full custody. I don't want to sway him away from his father either.

I want him to be able to enjoy his childhood without his parents' drama affecting his life, but knowing Paul, he's not going to let that happen.

I turn towards Bryce and smile. "I wanted to talk to you about your dad."

Bryce scowls back at me, his mouth pinched tight. "What about him?" His voice is cutting and sharp, obviously ready to defend his father against anything I'm about to say.

I close my eyes before looking back at him. "Remember when we went to that lawyer's office last week, and I said I had to talk to her about some stuff?" He nods, his expression getting even harder. "Your father has contacted a lawyer and is taking me to court."

"Good," he snaps, his hands balled into fists. "It's not right that you don't let me see him anymore, just because you don't like him. It's not fair."

My throat gets tight. Does my baby hate me? Has Paul already taken him from me? "Baby, I know you're angry, but you don't know the whole story."

"It doesn't even matter," he says, jumping up from his bed and pacing the room. "You're jealous of him. He knows it, and I know it."

My eyes fall close again, trying fight back the despair I feel, knowing that he will never fully understand. "Your father wants full custody of you."

Bryce's body freezes and he turns to face me. "What do you mean?"

I speak slowly so he can't mistake my meaning. "Your father thinks that you would be better off living with him, and only seeing me once in a while."

Bryce's head snaps back and his eyes blink rapidly. "You're lying. You're a liar."

"I'm not lying, Buddy. We've been to court already, and the judge said you can visit with your dad at a family centre, under supervision, until she can decide which of us you should live with. You're going to see him tomorrow."

He stares at me, his eyes unblinking as he takes in what I've just said. "Good," he barks. "I'm going to ask him myself, and he'll tell me the truth. Dads never lie to their kids."

It's my turn to stare at him. "Who told you that?"

"Dad did. Are you gonna tell me that's a lie too?"

I press my lips together and shake my head. It's no use talking to him right now. He's too angry, and isn't even listening to what I'm saying. I stand from the bed and skim my fingers through his hair. "Good night, Bud. I love you."

He doesn't respond. I walk out of his room feeling completely defeated. Bryce is a good kid, but he's wanted a father his whole life.

And now that he's finally got one, he's not going to let him go without a fight. I get that, I really do. I just wish I'd never responded to that Facebook message last year.

The phone rings just as I'm walking back into the kitchen. I look at the number and see that it's an unknown caller, so I let it go straight to voicemail. It's most likely Paul, and I can't deal with him right now.

A few seconds after the phone stops ringing, it alerts me of a new voicemail message. Putting in my password, I lift the phone to my ear.

"Ellen, just wanted to remind you again about the visitation tomorrow. It starts at four o'clock. It's best that you're not late. I get him for three hours, and you're not going to mess that up. Better yet, be late. It will look even better for me if you are. See you tomorrow."

I slam my phone down on the counter. I hate him! Why is he making everything so hard? Why, after all these years, does he want to take a child he never wanted in the first place?

Jase

THE TWO CHERRY wood caskets sit side by side, ready to be lowered into the ground. Looking around, I see the sad faces of just about everyone I know, all here to mourn the great loss we've all suffered. Even Ellen showed up in support of Charlie, but I haven't had the chance to talk to her. I don't even want to. I don't want to talk to anyone.

I haven't slept in three days, not since our entire world was rocked. Ryker and I had hauled ass to Gunner's house, terrified of what we would find there. I didn't know what to expect. I didn't even know what Bosco had said to Ryker on the phone. I'd just passed Gabby off to the others and followed my boy out to our bikes.

Bosco and Shank had been sitting on the front step of the tiny house, both shaky and looking a little green. Ryker took charge, heading right for them. "Show me," he demanded.

Bosco had stood and ran his fingers through his hair, warning us that it wasn't pretty. For the first time, I noticed the blood on his jeans and dark grey T-shirt.

Bosco was the first to go inside, followed by Ryker, me, then Shank. What we found inside will haunt me for the rest of my life. Two kitchen chairs sat back to back in the centre of the kitchen—Tess in one, Gunner in the other—both completely naked. Their wrists were bound together on each side, their hands holding tightly to each other, even in death. There were several signs that they'd been tortured before receiving a bullet directly to their brain.

Nobody knows all the gory details of what we saw that day, and nobody else ever will. The humiliation the pair suffered does not ever need to be spoken of, but every single person here knows that it was bad. It was only a few months ago that we had all gathered here, in this very same cemetery, to lay Mouse to rest. Being back here again is gut-wrenching.

At Mouse's funeral, Gunner had delivered an emotional speech about family and brotherhood. Now it's Ryker's turn to do the same for him. When it's Ryker's time to go to the head of the crowd, he presses a kiss against Charlie's hair and weaves his way to the back of both caskets.

While he's walking, Reaper leans in and whispers in my ear. "What the fuck is that evil cunt doing here?"

I look at him and frown, then follow the direction of his stare. His hate-filled glare is pinned directly on Anna, Charlie's sister, who's dressed in black and clutching Charlie's hand like a lifeline.

"She came in with the Montreal chapter. Said she wanted to be here for her sister."

"That stupid bitch has a lot of nerve showin' her face around here," he growls. "She's the one that started this whole fuckin' mess."

I don't get a chance to respond because Ryker begins speaking. "Gunner Monroe loved this club. He loved his kids, his wife, and the open road. I've known Gunner since I was just a kid, and one of the first things I learned about him was that you don't cross him—ever."

I can't listen. I know what he's going to say because I helped him write the damn thing. The fact is, I can't get the image of Gunner and Tess's dead bodies out of my head. More specifically, the image of their clasped hands in death, from my head.

Ryker is right. Gunner loved the shit out of his wife, and he did whatever he could to make that woman happy. There was no question that she loved him just as much. They'd met about ten years ago, but without knowing it, you'd swear they'd been together their entire lives. I'd never seen anything like it.

To be honest, I've never seen many functional relationships. Only two of the Kings had had old ladies when I was a kid, and those women didn't spend a lot of time at the clubhouse. My father never said much about my mother, but I knew she was a club whore who didn't even know she was pregnant until it was too late. My father took me from her when I was just a baby, after finding her strung out on crack, and me starving in my crib.

My dad never found an old lady, and had seemed perfectly happy with that. Until Gunner had met Tess, I'd never even seen a real relationship up close. Now they are everywhere. I look over at Charlie, her tear-filled eyes focused on her man as he gives a speech that I know is killing him to give. Ryker has changed so much since he met her. He's happy.

Beside Charlie is Laynie, her hands wrapped around Tease's bicep. Tease had been one of the most broken motherfuckers I'd ever seen. It had taken Laynie to pull his head out of his ass and see that his life wasn't over. He's still no fucking Rosie Sunshine, but you can see the love they share just by looking at them.

I see brothers from other chapters standing around, all focused on Ryker as he talks. Some of them are holding tight to the woman they love. Even Gunner's daughter, Gabby, and his son, Derrick, have someone with them, holding them up as they struggle through the pain.

My eyes move to Ellen. Her face is red and splotchy, her eyes full of tears as she listens to the eulogy. She looks beautiful. Her eyes meet mine from across the circle and she smiles a sad smile, using a tattered tissue to wipe her cheeks.

I want to comfort her. I want to be there for her as much as I want her to be there for me. She was wrong the other day. Cutting me out is not going to make that fucker go away. He's an asshole, and he's in it for the long haul. But I was wrong too. I'd walked away too easily. I didn't fight for her.

She turns her attention back to Ryker, but I keep my eyes on her. Ellen had sent me packing to save a fight with her ex, but what she doesn't know is that I'm going to help her fight this fight. It's time for me to stop fucking around and claim my woman.

Ellen

I'm turning off the lights and checking the locks, ready to turn in for the night when there's a knock on the door. My heart pounds out of control. It's eleven-thirty. Who would be knocking on my door at this hour? I can hardly breathe as I stalk quietly towards the door. Nothing good ever comes from late night callers.

Peeking through the window beside the door, I flick on the porch light and relief floods me when I see the leather cut. *Jase*. I reach for the locks and start to open the door. Why would Jase be here at this time of night?

I open the door, ready to give him hell for scaring the shit out of me, when I see his slumped shoulders and downcast face. "Jase?"

He raises his head slightly and looks up at me through his eyelashes. "Can we talk? It'll only take a minute."

I don't hesitate. He looks so lost, so alone. It breaks my heart. Stepping aside, I motion for him to come inside. I close the door and turn to see him running his fingers through his hair, his eyes flicking around the room.

Before I even get a chance to speak, he starts talking. "I'm sorry to just pop over here like this, especially this late at night, but I wanted to make sure your kid would be in bed. He is in bed, right?"

"Yeah, he's——"

"Good," he cuts me off. "I wanted to thank you for coming to Gunner and Tess's funeral today. I mean, I know you came to be there for Charlie, but it was really nice to see you there."

I don't speak. He looks to be contemplating his next words, so I remain silent, ready to listen.

"Nobody takes me seriously," he blurts. His feet start moving and I stand in place, watching him pace back and forth in front of me. "All my life, I've been the funny guy, the nice guy. The one everyone can count on to cheer them up, or show them a good time. I never even noticed it until recently. Not a single person in my life takes me seriously."

I don't know what to say. He's right, to the best of my knowledge. All I've ever heard about Jase are party stories, or tales of his sexual escapades, but never anything serious. Never anything to indicate that he was about anything but being the life of the party.

"The truth is, El," he turns and looks at me, "I'm tired of being that guy. I'm tired of being the guy everyone laughs at, the guy people tell stories about. But most of all, I'm tired of being the guy that's always alone." My heart clenches. "My dad died a few years back, did you know that?"

I shake my head.

"He got in a wreck driving up to see his buddies in Montreal. Died on the scene."

I reach out and place my hand on his arm. "I'm sorry, Jase."

He covers my hand with his and threads his fingers through mine. "You know what? It's fine. I've dealt with it. Me and my old man, we weren't the closest. He was okay, but we never really connected, ya know?" I give him a sad smile. "In every way imaginable, the Kings are my family. I grew up with those fuckers, but I'm learnin' more and more every day that none of them really know me, except for maybe Ryker. Maybe Reaper too, but nobody really *knows* me. They all see me as Jase the drinker, the partier, the joker...the womanizer." He lets out a brief laugh that doesn't contain an ounce of humour. "Hell, even Gunner thought I was a fuckin' joke."

"He didn't," I say, trying my best to soothe the ache I hear in his voice.

"He did," he whispers. "I'd never given him any reason to think anything else." Jase grabs my hand and pulls me towards the couch where he takes a seat and pulls me down beside him, turning our bodies so that our knees touch on one side, holding my hand in his.

The look on his face is determined.

"But you…" He pulls in a deep breath and squeezes my hand. "El, you make me want to prove to everyone that I'm not a joke. I don't want to be a joke anymore, or the life of the party." He grabs my chin and his eyes pin me in place. "What I want is to be yours. I want to be the one you count on, the one you turn to. I want to be with you so fuckin' bad, El."

My stomach sinks, my chest feeling tight and heavy. "Jase, you know I can't do that. I told you, the court—"

"I know what you said about the court, but what you don't know is that there is nothing on my record that the courts could use against me. I've never been charged with anything." He grins. "Not since before I turned eighteen, but those are stories for later."

I stare back at him incredulously. "How is that possible?"

He holds his hands out and smirks. "Please, like I'd ever get caught." His smirk fades and his face grows serious. "The truth is they just can't nail me with anything. They can, and do try, trust me. I get hauled in once in a while, we all do, but they have nothing they can use to make anything stick. The only thing they can prove about me is that I'm a motorcycle mechanic. I'm clean, El."

I bite at the inside of my cheek, my mind racing through all of the things he's just said, and what it could mean for us. "Why me?" I blurt out. "Why not one of the whores at the clubhouse, or one of the hundreds of other women that throw themselves at you all the time. What makes you want me?"

He blows out a breath and shrugs. "There's just something about you that draws me to you. Babe, I just want a chance to get to know you. I want to get to know your kid, even if he doesn't seem to like me all that much. I want to be there for you while you go through this shit with his dad. I want to be there to help you put that fucker in his place, so he stops pushin' you around and scarin' you. For the first time, El, I want to take the time to start something new, something good. It's the only thing I've thought about since the first time I saw you."

A tear rolls down my cheek. "I want that too," I whisper, "but I'm scared."

His arms wrap around me and he pulls me into a tight hug. "I know, baby," he says into my hair. "I know you are, but this…what we're startin'…it's gonna be fuckin' incredible. You wait and see."

Jase

I WATCH ELLEN'S face as she takes in everything I've said, wanting more than anything for her to believe every word, to be the first person to take me seriously, believing me when I say that I want this—that I want her.

Her expression gives away nothing as her eyes stare intently into mine. I stare back at her, an empty feeling forming in my stomach. What was I thinking? This woman has done nothing but tell me to get lost, and here I am, once again, practically begging her to take a chance on me. I feel like a fool. I open my mouth to speak, just as Ellen stands up.

I don't take my eyes off her as she reaches out her hand and says, "Come with me."

I take her hand, the rhythm of my heart beating completely out of time, and I stand. She turns, pulling me behind her and walking towards the hallway, where I can only assume the bedrooms are. We enter a small bedroom, decorated in black, white, and lime green. The walls are covered in framed pictures.

She walks right up to the bed and turns, looking me directly in the eyes, and peels her T-shirt up and over her head, revealing the lacy pink bra underneath. The need I see in her eyes nearly matches my own, and for the first time in my life, I'm nervous. For the first time in my life, this means something.

"I can't believe I'm about to say this, but this isn't what I want." I pull away from her, putting some distance between myself and her half naked body. "I want you, El, and that means all of you. I want to experience a life with you in every way, not just sex. I want to be *with* you."

"That's what I want too," she admits. I'm floored. My body hums with excitement, causing my head and my dick to tell me two entirely different things. "Jase, do you have any idea how long it's been for me?"

I shake my head. The truth is, I don't want to know anything about the last time Ellen had sex. The idea of some other dude running his fingers over her creamy smooth skin makes me want to kill him.

"Four years," she says, her voice barely above a whisper. "I've been on a few dates since then, but as I get older, the guys I meet are just not what I'm looking for. And I have never brought a man around Bryce."

I move closer and run my finger from the base of her throat, along the firm round hills of her breast until I get to the trim of her bra. Leaning forward, I press my lips to hers, my tongue sliding along hers, reveling in the taste of this woman.

"Good," I whisper, my hand coming up and palming her breast, giving it a gentle squeeze. "I'm glad."

Releasing her breast, I trail my fingers even lower, skimming my fingertips along her belly and slipping a single finger inside the waistband of her thin cotton pajama pants. She gasps softly into my mouth, clasping her hands onto the back of my neck, deepening our kiss.

Slowly, I dip my hand inside until I feel the small tuft of trimmed hair between her legs. My heart crashes inside my chest, and I have to focus on my breathing to keep it from getting out of my control.

My finger finally finds her warm heat, and she lets out a sharp cry as I dip it all the way down to her wet centre, collecting the juices that are soaking into her panties. Bringing the tip of my finger back up, I circle the hard little nub that brings her so much pleasure, I have to wrap my free arm around her waist to keep her steady.

"You like that, baby?" I rasp. She whimpers and nods, her mouth nipping and licking at mine. "Pull your tits out, El."

My cock strains against my zipper as I feel her body tremble in my arms and hear the sounds she's making as I draw out her pleasure. She pulls down one cup, and then the other, proudly displaying them just for me. They're fucking perfect.

Each one is creamy and smooth, and just a little more than a handful. My mouth waters, wanting to taste her perfect pink nipple. Reaching down, I press one finger, then two, deep inside her pussy, hooking them in the perfect place while pressing the heel of my hand against her clit.

She slams her mouth to mine to muffle her moans of pleasure. I break our kiss and move my mouth down to her tits to suck on her nipple, flicking it with my tongue. She cries into her palm, and I feel her pussy clench tighter around my fingers.

Pulling away, I look up at her and can barely speak. "Come for me, El."

Her hips sway along with the rhythm of my hand. I feel her pussy grow more wet with every stroke, but it's not until I lean forward and sink my teeth into her nipple, just hard enough to cause a little pain, that her body convulses, my name falling from her lips.

Pulling back, I look and admire the pink flush that spreads across every inch of her skin. She yanks me back, slamming her lips onto mine as she fumbles awkwardly with my belt. "We need to stop," I say.

She grins and grabs my face, lips aiming for me once more, but I pull back, putting some distance between us. "I mean it, babe. We need to stop. As much as I want to finish what we've started, it's not the right time."

She folds her arms over her heaving chest, suddenly embarrassed. Taking her chin between my thumb and forefinger, I tilt her face up to mine and press a soft kiss to her swollen lips. "My dick is going to be more pissed than either one of us, trust me." I grin as she giggles and fold her in my arms. "Let me take you out the day after tomorrow. We'll do dinner, a bike ride, and maybe, just maybe, I'll even buy you flowers or some shit."

"I'd like that."

"Good. It's a date."

Ellen

The next morning, I'm pouring my coffee just as Bryce walks into the kitchen. His hair is a mess, and his pajamas are rumpled from a good night's sleep. "Morning, Bud. How'd you sleep?"

"Good," he mumbles as he reaches for the cereal. I grin wide. For the first time in a long time, so had I. And if Bryce slept well, that means he didn't hear what was going on in my room.

Jase's visit last night had changed everything. It had changed my mind about finally giving him a chance to prove that he's serious about me, no matter how much that terrifies me. I'm no fool, and I'm still cautious about giving him my complete trust, but we'll take it slow and see what happens.

His visit also means that I have to come clean to Bryce about who he is, and what he means to me. He talks to his father, and I know that it'll get brought up. I don't want Paul to think I'm hiding something, and I want him to know that he can't push me around and dictate who I can and cannot date. Besides, Bryce is a smart kid. There's no way I could date Jase without him knowing something was going on.

"Bryce, I need to talk to you about something." His eyes lift from the iPad game he's playing as he scoops Lucky Charms into his mouth. "I'm going out tonight. I already texted Brit, but if you want to to go to Jimmy's instead, I can call his mom and see if that would be okay."

His eyes narrow and his freckled nose scrunches up. "No thanks. Jimmy isn't my friend anymore."

"What? Why not?" Jimmy and Bryce have been friends since kindergarten. They do everything together. His mom's a nurse too, over at the General Hospital. Through the years, we've helped each other out a lot, taking each other's boys so we could do simple things, like go Christmas shopping, or out to a movie.

" 'Cause he's a dork," he replies, squinting his eyes, daring me to argue.

"That's not nice, Bryce. We don't talk about people that way, especially not our friends. Did you guys get in a fight?"

"No, Mom. He's just a loser, and I don't want to be friends with him anymore. Where are you going?"

I ignore the change of subject, thinking it best to drop it and see if the boys work it out for themselves. I don't like to meddle in his life more than I need to, opting to let him figure things out as he goes. I only offer advice when I feel I need to.

I take a deep breath and decide to just lay it out there. "I'm going on a date." He blinks back at me. "Remember that man I was talking to out front last week?"

"The biker guy?" he asks, his expression one of disgust.

"Yep. His name is Jase, not biker guy. Anyways, he's my friend and he asked me out. I said yes, and I'm looking forward to spending some time with him."

"I don't like it," he declares, his chin held high.

"I hate to say it kid, but tough." I watch as his mouth turns down in a frown. Bryce isn't used to me making decisions without at least asking his opinion. "I'm your mom, and you're my kid. It's my job to make the choices for this family, and it's yours to accept them. I would never do anything that would be dangerous for you, and you know I love you more than anything, but I have a life to live, so you're just gonna have to accept that too."

He opens his mouth to argue, but I hold up my hand. "I know you called your father the last time he was here, and your father said you seemed afraid of Jase, but you need to know that he's not a scary man—he's a good man."

He wrinkles his nose again. "I wasn't afraid. I told him 'cause he asked if you have any boyfriends." I shake my head. Yet another way Paul is manipulating our son so he can win this case against me. "I didn't like him, but I wasn't scared."

"Why didn't you like him?"

"He was practically making out with you on the sidewalk in the middle of our neighborhood. It was gross."

"Oh, buddy," I laugh. "We weren't even kissing. And you should have told me when I talked to you about the way you treated him." Bryce just shrugs. Reaching across the table, I place my hand on his. "I'm not going to run out and marry this guy, Bryce. I just want to get to know him, let him get to know me. If things work out, and I decide it's worth it, then maybe he can get to know you, and you know him. You need to stop worrying so much about this stuff and just be a kid, okay?"

He thinks on it for a moment before he nods. "Good," I say with a wink. "So, if Brit can babysit, you'll be hanging out with her for the night. I'll leave money for pizza."

Brit is Brittany, a sixteen-year-old girl from down the street who babysits for me from time to time. She's a good kid, and Bryce always enjoys it when she comes over.

I don't miss Bryce's grin as he rinses out his bowl and puts it in the dishwasher. "What's so funny?" I ask.

"Nothing. I'm just glad it's Brit coming over and not Mrs. Cameron from down the street." He wags his eyebrows at me. "Brit's hot."

I gasp and shake my head as he hurries out of the room. At what age do you stop having a babysitter take care of your kid? I'm starting to wonder if the answer to that is, when they start thinking they're hot.

Jase

RYKER BANGS THE gavel down on the long wooden table, causing every man in the room to stop talking and look in his direction. "This fuckin' sucks," he declares. "As VP of this club, I knew that being the one to carry on our meetings without the Prez was a duty I'd have to do, but I never once dreamed that it would be for this reason."

Several of the guys nod their heads, while others lower them sadly. "This club has been shaken harder than it's ever been shaken before, and now we need to shake it up even more. We need to have a vote, maybe rearrange some positions. So, I'm just gonna dive right in and start at the top and work my way down. Everyone ready?"

Murmurs of agreement fill the room.

"Nominations for chapter president. Call them out now."

Everyone looks around the room, but no one says a word until Reaper finally breaks the silence. "I nominate you, Ryker."

Ryker nods. "Thank you, Reap. Anyone else?" His words are met with silence. Every man in this room knows that Ryker is exactly what this club needs—who *we* need. "All in favor?" One by one, we go around the room, ending in a unanimous round of 'ayes.'

"All opposed?" Silence.

Ryker stares back at us and lifts his fist to his chest. "Thank you, brothers. Gunner pulled this club out of some pretty heavy shit. He was an amazing president, and I will do everything I can to do him, and all of you, proud." He's quiet for a moment before he continues, "So with me moving spots, now we need to elect a VP. Call out your nominations now."

I open my mouth, ready to call out Tease's name, when I hear my own name called out three different times. Ryker, Tease, and Slots have all nominated me to be the club VP. I look to Ryker with wide eyes, only to see him smiling. "All in favor?" More 'ayes.'

"All opposed?" Silence.

"Congratulations, brother." He reaches up and rips off the VP patch from his own vest, sliding it across the table to me. My fingers wrap around the small piece of material and my heart races. I was just elected vice fucking president of the very club I thought didn't take me seriously.

I can barely speak, and my words come out strangled, "Thank you, everyone."

"Reaper is our current Sergeant at Arms. All in favor of keeping him there?" We all ring out with a resounding round of 'ayes.'

"All opposed?" Silence.

Ryker goes through the same thing with the positions of secretary and treasurer, both members continuing on. Ryker motions for the chair to his left, indicating for me to take the official seat for the vice president of the club. Standing, I walk around the table and sit beside Ryker, who then claps me on the back and turns to face the others.

"Now we need to figure some shit out. I'm not gonna pussyfoot around the issue. We know who killed Gunner and Tess—they left their calling card there to make sure we did, but here's the deal. The Crips are a huge gang, and much bigger than the Kings. If we go to war with those bastards, it will never end."

"So we let it slide?" Tease snarls. "Let those fuckers get away with torturing and killing our club president and his old lady?"

Ryker holds up his hand. "That's not what I said. We will retaliate, and they will pay, but we need to be smart about this. If we enter into a war, none of us will ever be safe in this city—not us, not our women, and not our children. Those bastards are like cockroaches—they're everywhere, and they're hard to kill. This fuckin' city is infested with them, so we need to plan. We need to play this smart, and we need to move fast. They fucked with the wrong club, and they're about to learn that shit the hard way." He looks around at us in a way that reminds me so much of Gunner. "So I want to hear your ideas. I know every one of you crazy bastards have secretly been plotting how you want to deal with them, so lay it on me. What've ya got?"

We spend the next three hours in discussions. We go around the room, presenting ideas (really fucked up ideas), and break them down, figuring out what will work and what won't. It's exhausting, but it makes us all feel like we're finally going to get some justice for Gunner and Tess.

Watching Ryker lead the meeting fills me with pride. He settles arguments and keeps the conversation going so that no one feels like they haven't been heard. My boy is going to kick this job's ass, and with me by his side, we'll be unstoppable.

Ellen

I'm sitting in the waiting room of the courthouse, doing my best to avoid Paul's glare, when the bailiff emerges and announces that the judge would like to speak with both Paul and me. My knees are weak as I stand from the bench and move towards him, pleading with God to make this turn out okay. Why does the judge want to see us this time? Has she reached her decision?

Stella stands behind a long table at the left side of the room, motioning for me to join her. I watch with wide eyes as Paul strides confidently to the table where his lawyer stands, waiting for him. "You okay?" Stella whispers when I reach her.

My entire body shakes, my limbs seeming to have a mind of their own. I look back at her and nod, terrified that if I try to speak, the scream I'm holding back will come bubbling up to the surface.

"You may be seated," the judge declares, placing a small pair of spectacles low on her nose. "When it comes to the case of Chapman vs. McGrath, I have reached my decision." I take a deep breath and stare up at her, hot tears forming in my eyes. The next words out of the judge's mouth are going to affect my son and me for the next seven years.

"Miss McGrath, please stand." My knees tremble as I stand from the chair with Stella's assistance, gripping tight to the edge of the table. "You had your child very young. I understand that your family did not help in any way, is this true?"

"Yes, Your Honor," I squeak out.

"I also understand that you had some help from a friend and her family, and that you were able to support your child for ten years without any help from Mr. Chapman. You even put yourself through school to be a nurse in that time. Is this true?"

"Yes." My heart lifts slightly, and hope starts to bloom deep in my belly.

The judge turns to Paul. "Mr. Chapman, please stand."

Their chairs scrape across the floor as Paul and his lawyer stand, Paul's face intent on the judge, but the smug look he once had is gone.

"Mr. Chapman, you were aware of the birth of your son, Bryce. Am I correct in that statement?"

"Yes, Your Honor."

"You did not try to contact him or Miss McGrath until after the child's tenth birthday. Is this also true?"

"Yes, Your Honor, but I—"

"I'm talking, Mr. Chapman. I will thank you to just answer the questions with a yes or a no, unless otherwise instructed. Am I clear?"

"Yes," he says, his jaw set in a hard line.

"I believe that this is a case of two young children, getting themselves into trouble and creating a child that neither of them were ready for. Mr. Chapman took the cowards way out, and avoided the child entirely, while Miss McGrath worked hard, making sure she could provide a good life for her son." I take a deep breath, doing my best to hide my growing smile. "That being said, I think that unless the parent is unfit in some way, I see no reason why a child should be kept from them. Mr. Chapman, while I see evidence that you are indeed a difficult man, I see nothing that says you are abusive. On those grounds, I award you visitation rights to your son."

Conflicting emotions rage war inside my heart. I knew that he would win the right to see Bryce, and it's much better than him getting full or even joint custody, but knowing that it's legal now, that I have to comply with a judge's order and let Bryce see Paul, makes me nauseous.

Paul's smug face turns to me and smirks, clearly gloating in the fact that he won even this small victory. He continues to smirk at me the entire time the judge lays out the schedule. Every second weekend, every other holiday, and two weeks in the summer, Bryce will be sent to be with Paul.

"Mr. Chapman," the judge barks. "Your smug attitude is indicative of what I meant when I said you are a difficult man." Paul stops smirking and looks over at the judge.

"Sorry, Your Honor."

"During the ten years of your son's life that you missed, as well as the one you were present for, Miss McGrath has supported your son entirely on her own. That will not do, Mr. Chapman. I find that you owe Miss McGrath eleven years in back child support payments, as well as monthly payments from this day forward. I will get your lawyer to present the paperwork for you to sign."

Paul's panicked eyes dart from his lawyer, to the judge, then to me. I almost feel bad for him. That's a lot of money. But then I remember my enormous student loans, and Bryce's need for braces. Not to mention his meager college fund that could use some serious beefing up. That makes me feel better.

Jase

I RIDE BEHIND Ryker in our new formation, still trying to get used to my new title and place in the hierarchy of the club. Earlier today, Ryker had sent two of our prospects out, intent on hunting down a couple of low-level Crips. It didn't take them long to find two young guys, barely out of their teens, walking downtown.

They'd drawn guns on our guys, but thankfully, instead of shooting, they'd listened to what they had to say. Bosco had explained to them that our club prez wanted a meeting with their leader, Face. We wanted to work out an arrangement. Bosco told them to meet us tonight at the same lot we'd shot up their men a few months ago, when fighting against the Devil's Rejects.

After a quick phone call to their leader, we had ourselves a date.

Reaper and Tease had gone ahead of us, wanting to beat our enemies to the meeting spot. It's the perfect place because it's secluded and deserted, and there are lots of places to hide, which is exactly why we sent our two most ruthless men to sweep the place and lie in wait.

As agreed, we pull into the parking lot a full ten minutes after the

Crips were due to arrive. There's a large man standing in front, two directly behind him, and at least thirty more men, forming the rest of their crew. It was agreed there'd be no weapons, but I don't miss the baseball bats and crowbars in the hands of several of the Crips.

As a group, we park our bikes and form our own group with Ryker in front, facing the Crips' leader, me and Slots behind him, and the rest of our guys put us at a group of eighteen. I don't take my eyes off their leader, who cracks his knuckles and sneers at Ryker.

"You got a lot of balls demanding a meeting with me, grease monkey," Face sneers. My eyes scan the crowd in front of us, watching for any sudden movements. We're surrounded by ten, very large shipping containers, and I know that directly behind me, Reaper and Tease are camped out on one of them, Reaper's silenced sniper rifle ready to go when needed. Ryker's plan is risky at best, but if it works, our war with the Crips will be over, and they'll know not to fuck with the Kings in the future.

Ryker holds up his hand. "We're here to talk truce," he states.

I watch as Face's expression goes from surprised to amused in an instant. Laughter booms from his throat, the others in his group laughing it up right alongside him. Suddenly, the two men directly behind him, crumple to the ground, with perfect round holes placed directly in the centre of their foreheads.

The laughter stops and every man, Crips and Kings, pull out their pieces, aiming and ready to fire at will. Face shakes with rage, his skin flushed and his eyes wide. "What the fuck are you doing? You call this a truce?" His gun is directed at Ryker. I guess none of us wanted to show up without being strapped.

Ryker's gun doesn't waver as it points directly back at him. "We just killed your two best men. You killed our prez and his old lady. A life for a life. I think this could make us about even now, wouldn't you say?"

Face's eyes scan the shipping containers behind us, his eyes moving rapidly. "If you're looking for your men, our guys have got them tied up in the back," Ryker says matter of factly.

"What are you proposing?"

Ryker lowers his gun, motioning for the rest of us to do the same.

We do, but we don't put them away, keeping them in our hands and ready. "With Gunner gone, I'm prez now. I want to make some changes—big changes. I wanna go clean."

Face eyes him up and down before lowering his gun, motioning for the rest of his men to do the same. They do, but I don't miss the one guy directly across from me who looks more pissed than any of the others. It's the guy from the Escalade, the one that shot at the sign on the compound. He's wiry and small, and his handshakes as he grips the butt of the gun tightly in his hand. His knuckles are white as he stares at Ryker.

"I know you're pissed about what happened with your men a few months ago," Ryker continues.

"Yeah, you fucking ambushed 'em," the angry one yells. I watch as Face turns to him and makes a hand gesture, calming the guy down, but only slightly.

"You're right," Ryker says. "We did, but our fight was with the Devil's Rejects, not the Crips. We just finished our war with them, and we're not looking for another one with you."

"I can't just let that fuckin' go, man," Face says. "I can't forget that you killed a bunch of my boys."

Ryker sighs. "Part of goin' clean is gettin' out of the weed business. We grow it, we transport it, and we sell it. We want out. I'm willing to hand it over to you, sixty percent of our grow ops, and let you have them with the condition that this war is over."

Face blinks. "And the other forty?"

"The Bloods." Angry rumbles come from the Crips. Apparently, not all of them like that part at all. "Look, man, the Bloods have been good to us, and they're getting the rest. I won't budge on this."

Face's jaw clenches as he weighs his options. "What's the catch?"

Ryker smiles, but his eyes are hard. "We fight."

Face scoffs. "Are you fuckin' kidding me, man? You want to fight me?"

Ryker nods and stuffs his gun back into it's holster, making a point of showing it to Face. "You beat me, you get the weed, and a truce."

"And if I lose?"

"We continue our war, and the Bloods get it all."

Face throws his head back and laughs. "You hear that boys? The biker wants to fight. Let's show these greasy fuckers how we do things."

"What?" the guy with the teardrop tat yells as Face starts pushing up his sleeves. "A deal? What about my brother?"

Face turns and glares at the guy before turning back to Ryker, his fists raised and ready to go. Just as Ryker's steps closer, I see the guy hold his gun out, pointing it straight at Ryker. He takes two giant steps, nearly closing the distance between them.

Lifting my own gun, I aim a shot right at him, hiding my grin when he jumps back.

My shot hits the ground directly in front of him, putting a burn mark on the toe of his boot from where the bullet grazed it.

Nobody moves. Even the Kings are surprised. I guess not all of them knew that I'm a crack shot.

That's one thing my dad and I used to do together when he did spend time with me. We shot guns.

Face steps forward and grabs his man by the back of the shirt, yanking him back and letting him fall to the ground on his ass. "You think you know what's best for my guys, Colt?"

"These fuckers killed my brother! You said you'd fuckin' handle them, and now you're fist fighting for a fuckin' weed deal?" Colt stands and puts his gun back in his pocket. "That's bullshit, man, and you know it."

I can only see Face from behind, so I'm not quite sure what's happening until his giant fist pulls back and punches forward, slamming it into Colt's nose. The blow causes him to fall right back down on his ass once more. "You don't ever question me, you dumbass," is all Face says before turning back to Ryker. "Let's do this."

Ryker grins a wolfish smile and raises his fists. The two men square off, and then it's on. Fists fly, and the sound of flesh hitting bone barely registers above the yelling of the men as everyone rallies in a circle, cheering on their leaders. It's like being at a high school brawl all over again.

I stand by, watching as Ryker carefully aims his punches, taking an occasional hit himself, but I'm not worried. Ryker is one of the scrappiest motherfuckers I know. I've never known him to lose a fight in his life, and he's been in his fair share of 'em.

Face keeps throwing punches, landing fewer and fewer as his anger grows. Ryker, on the other hand, lands every blow. Face's face is almost unrecognizable, but he doesn't give up. "Crazy fucker," he grunts out, swinging another misplaced punch at Ryker. "I should've fuckin' killed you too."

Ryker's knee comes up and crashes into Face's gut, anger finally starting to show on his face. Face falls to his knees, his arms wrapped around his torso, but still he doesn't shut up. "You fight like your old Prez," he says on a gasp, grinning up at Ryker with two missing teeth visible through his deranged smile. "That fucker fought like a son of a bitch. Took six of us to tie him and that old bitch down. She was a fuckin' wildcat, if ya know what I mean."

Rage burns through me, and I'm seething. I want to get my own hits in on that piece of shit. Before I finish the thought, Ryker slams his knee into Face's nose, sending him flying to the ground, barely conscious. I love the sound of Face's nose being crushed.

"Jinks, Toro, Jolly," Ryker calls out over the anxious crowd. Nobody moves. What the fuck is he doing? Ryker pulls out his gun and presses it against the side of Face's head. "I won't fuckin' ask again, you sons of bitches. Jinks, Toro, Jolly! Unless you wanna watch your leader's brains get blown out, I suggest you step forward so we can have a chat."

A low murmur makes its way across the Crips. Three men step into the circle, and before any of us can react, Ryker swings his gun up and points it at the three men. "You were three of the six that killed our Prez." The men say nothing, but their anger is obvious.

Ryker's nod is so slight; I barely catch it before he fires. I also hear the silent ping of Reaper's sniper rifle come from above us, and all three men fall to the ground. What the fuck just happened?

Ryker turns and points his gun back at Face, who lays on the ground, his mouth full of blood. "You stupid fuck. You think this is gonna end shit? You've just declared—"

He doesn't get a chance to finish 'cause Ryker puts a bullet in his head. Suddenly, guns are pointing in all directions, everyone screaming at one another. Just when I'm sure the shooting's about to start, one man from the Crips steps forward, his hands held high in the air, showing that he has no gun.

"Who the fuck are you?" Ryker calls over the yelling.

"Jasper. My name is Jasper. Crips, put down your weapons." One by one, the Crips reluctantly lower their guns, giving their attention to this man, Jasper. "I'm interested in taking your deal," he says, his hands still high as he looks to Ryker.

"Do you have that authority?"

Jasper nods to Face's dead body. "I do now."

Ryker studies the man with piercing scrutiny, his gun pointed directly at him. After a long and tense moment, he seems to come to a decision. "Sixty percent of the weed, and there's no further fallback with my men."

Jasper nods. "You have a deal."

Ryker lowers his gun, and one by one, everyone else holsters their weapons, except for the Kings.

As he and Jasper hammer out the details, the skinny guy, Colt, glares at me, but I don't mind. An admirer is an admirer, and I don't discriminate.

When the meeting concludes, the Crips reluctantly begin making their way to their vehicles. I watch as the last one drives away with Colt in the back.

He looks directly at me and holds out his fingers like a gun, pretending to pull back the hammer, then BAM, just like he did before.

Once they're gone, Reaper and Tease climb down from the top of the shipping containers. We all look to Ryker. I know I'm not the only one wondering, so I ask, "What the fuck just happened?"

Ryker turns to me and grins. "It worked."

"What the fuck is that supposed to mean?"

"Jasper reached out to me, said he knew exactly who was involved in killing Gunner and Tess. He hasn't been happy with the way Face and his cronies have been running things, so we came up with a plan that suited both our needs. He got to take over the Crips, and we got the fuckers that killed two of our own. We're one step closer to getting clean, we ended the war with the Crips before it started, and we gave Jasper a chance to turn things around for his gang." He lifts his finger and motions for the prospects to get to work, cleaning up the carnage.

Reaper stares at him incredulously. "How the fuck did you know it would even work?"

Ryker shrugs his shoulders. "I didn't. But fuck, I'm glad it did."

Ellen

It's not even ten o'clock when I decide that it's time for me to go to bed. It's been a long day, and I'm both mentally and physically drained. Not only did court not go exactly as I'd planned, but I'd also come home to an angry message on my voicemail from Jimmy's mom. Apparently, Bryce had shoved him to the ground today while they were at school. Jimmy was upset, but refused to tell the school because he didn't want Bryce to get in trouble.

What am I going to do? Bryce isn't a bully. He's always made friends so easily. I know things with Paul have been stressful for him, but is that enough to cause such a huge shift in personality when it comes to people other than me?

I'd attempted to talk to Bryce about it, but he was rude and snarky, which only pissed me off. He's lost access to his game systems for a couple of weeks, and I still haven't gotten to the bottom of anything. Maybe it's time for me to seek outside help. A therapist might be able to connect with Bryce about what's going on with him better than I can.

I lie in bed for two hours, tossing and turning, while my mind races through everything that happened today. It's after midnight when my phone vibrates with a text message lighting up my screen.

Jase: You awake?

I smile as my heart soars. I plug in four different messages and delete them before finally deciding on one.

Me: Yes.

Short, simple, and to the point. There's no need for him to know that he makes my knees go weak with a single text.

Jase: Can I call you? I need to hear your voice.

A giggle bursts from my lips, and I clap a hand over my mouth. Girls that giggle annoy the shit out of me, and I refuse to be that girl. But no matter how much I try to hold it in, I can't deny the excitement that courses through me at his words.

Me: Of course.

My phone vibrates again, this time showing me that I'm getting a call. I answer it on the first ring. "Hey," I breathe out.

I hear him let out a long sigh. "Hey, El. Do you know how much better I feel just from hearing your voice?"

I do. I know exactly how he feels, because I feel the same. I miss him. I don't know how, or even why. I just saw him yesterday, and it's not like we spend a lot of time together. I don't get it, but I like it. "Bad day?" I ask.

He blows out a breath. "The worst. What about you? How did court go?"

"Not like I'd hoped, but it could've been worse. Why was yours so terrible?"

"Just club shit that I can't talk about."

"Can't or won't?" I ask, wishing I could know more about what has him so down.

"Both, babe. Unfortunately, that's not ever gonna change when it comes to my club, and if that bothers you…well, it'll suck, but my club is my family. There's always gonna be club shit that I can't and won't talk to you about."

I knew this already. Charlotte's talked about it before, about not knowing being a good thing sometimes. "Okay," I reply. "I get it, but I wish I could make you feel better." The noise I hear coming from the other end is distracting. "Where are you? It sounds like you're in a bar."

"I'm at home," he grumbles, clearly irritated. "I live at the club-house. There's a party going on down the hall. They happen every night here."

"That has to get old," I say. I like my peace and quiet, and especially my privacy. I couldn't handle being in the middle of a giant party every night.

"Oh, it has," he chuckles.

"So why do you live there?"

"It's a long story."

"Well, I can't sleep, and you can't sleep, so maybe if you tell me the story, it will bore me enough that I'll finally pass out."

His laughter makes me feel warm, all the way down to my toes. "You're kind of a jerk, El. Do you know that?"

"I do," I laugh. "Now tell me."

He chuckles again and starts his story. He tells me a little more about his dad and how his mom was a club whore that never wanted him. He tells me about his dad's affliction for being promiscuous, and that's all he ever saw as a kid, which was how he believed relationships were until Gunner met Tess. He tells me how he'd never even considered moving out of clubhouse until he met me.

"Why me?" I ask softly. I know I've asked this before, but it's something that I just can't seem to wrap my head around.

"You make me want more in life, El. For the first time, I'm looking at my life, and I realize that what I have is never gonna be good for a family man. And that's what I want, ya know—a family." My heart races. "Someday," he rushes out. "That's also something I've never considered until I met you."

"Wow," I breathe. "And what is it you expect a family man should have?"

"A house," he answers. "A job he can be proud of, and a decent bank account so he can buy his lady nice shit."

"I'm not looking for any of that, Jase."

"I know, but you deserve it."

He sounds like he's put some serious thought into this, and that makes me smile. The truth is, I hadn't even thought about Jase much beyond our date tomorrow. I don't like to get my hopes up, and he's not known for being monogamous. I figure if I can keep my expectations of him low, that leaves less room for him to hurt me.

"Well, now that I've scared the shit out of you, I'm gonna go turn in. I'll see you tomorrow."

"Okay. Good night, Jase."

"Good night, baby."

I put my phone back on the nightstand and let my mind go over our conversation. I'm stunned and beside myself. I never would have imagined that Jase would ever be serious about me. Of course this makes me happy, almost as much as it terrifies me.

What if I give Jase this chance and he hurts me? What if works out? Could he accept Bryce, or Bryce accept him?

After another hour, I finally drift off to sleep, the sound of Jase's voice echoing in my mind. *You make me want more in life, El.* God. He seems almost too good to be true.

Jase

I WALK UP the front steps to Ellen's house for our date, my heart thudding in my chest. I have a lot of experience with women, but when I really think about it, I don't know much about them at all, besides how to please them in bed.

I ring the doorbell and wait. When the door swings open, I look down and my stomach turns when I see Ellen's kid. I have even less knowledge of kids than I do women. He holds the door open, but doesn't step aside for me to enter, and he doesn't say a word, choosing instead to look me up and down, making sure I know that he doesn't like what he sees. Who the fuck is this kid?

"Is your mom home?" I ask, starting to feel a little uncomfortable under his gaze.

"What happened to your ear?" he asks.

I fucking knew it. Fucking Reaper! He told me that it was just a little graze, and that nobody would ever notice, but this kid doesn't miss it. I'm gonna kick that hairy giant's ass next time I see him. I lift my hand and skim my fingers along the tip of my ear, right where the bullet took off a chunk, leaving me disfigured.

"I was shot."

His face twists into a sour expression and his head jerks back. "In the ear? You can't get shot in the ear." He snorts, shaking his head in disgust. I don't even get a chance to respond before Ellen walks up next to him.

She places her hand on her son's shoulder and steers him out of the way. "Jase, come in." I step inside, brushing my shoulder against her as I pass. She smells like vanilla. "I see you've met Bryce."

"Yeah," I reply, raising my brow at him. He shrugs like he's bored and walks away.

"Bryce can be a little...difficult, but he's a good kid. He's not used to me going on a date."

I lean in, kissing her on the cheek. "It's fine. He seems cool." Remembering the flowers in my hand, I hold them out to her, suddenly feeling a little foolish. "These are for you."

Her cheeks turn a gorgeous shade of pink as she smiles, causing her eyes to shine happily at me. My chest aches as she reaches for them. "Thank you," she whispers.

I reach out and wrap my hand around the back of her neck, pulling her closer and ghosting my lips over hers. "You're welcome," I whisper back before I cover her mouth with mine.

She moans softly, her knees bending as she leans into me, holding the flowers out to the side. When I finally break our kiss and look down at her, she blinks up. "You're lethal."

"And you're beautiful." Her pink flush gets even deeper.

I wait by the door while she puts her flowers in water, goes over things one last time with the babysitter, and then we're off to the restaurant. I'd looked into where to take her, but finally settled on The Angry Pelican. It's a popular little bar and grill right downtown, with a nice patio that overlooks the water. It's perfect for a first date, and close to where I want to take her next.

"This place is awesome," Ellen says as she glances around. The patio is busy, but not crowded, and the sun is still shining high in the sky, warming us against the breeze coming off the river. "Have you been here before?" she asks.

I shake my head. "Never."

"How'd you find it?"

"Actually, Charlie recommended it. Her and Ryk come here sometimes. She said that you'd love it."

"You got dating advice from Charlie?"

I smirk and I know that my cheeks are turning pink. "I did. I had no clue where to take you. I've never been on a date before."

She's just taking a sip of her drink and spits it all over the table. "What?" she chokes, wiping the water off her chin with a linen napkin. "That can't be true."

"El, I won't lie. I've been with a lot of women, but I didn't date a single one of them. I wanted one thing from them, and one thing only."

Ellen slaps her hands over her ears. "Okay! I don't want to hear the details." She lowers her hands, reaching out to place her hand on my arm. "I'm honored to be your first date."

The waitress appears with our food and we dig in. The food is delicious. Charlie was right about this place. We chat as we eat, Ellen talking a little about her job, and telling me some funny stories about some of the people she works with. I tell her a little about building choppers, and how I want to start a business doing just that.

She seems genuinely interested, and when I tell her about the chopper I just sold, she looks at me with an expression I've never before seen aimed at me...pride. Ellen's proud of me, and impressed that I can build a motorcycle from scratch.

After the waitress takes our plates and leaves me with the bill, Ellen takes my hand. "This has been an amazing date, Jase. Thank you for being a pushy bastard and not taking no for an answer."

I grin back at her. "My pleasure, but the fun's not over yet."

Ellen

"Where are we going?" I ask, looking around at all the beautiful old stone buildings. This is a very historic part of the city, and not somewhere you would normally see a biker out for an evening stroll with his lady.

"Almost there," he says, squeezing my hand and smiling. I love his smile. I've spent a little time around the Kings, and one thing I've noticed is that these guys don't do a whole lot of smiling. Jase smiles all the time, and it's blinding.

Up ahead is a small gathering of people, standing on the sidewalk out in front of one of the old buildings. "Are we protesting something," I tease.

He laughs. "No. Charlie had some other advice, other than restaurants."

"Sounds like I need to start dating Charlie."

"I don't share, but I'm always in favor of a little girl-on-girl action if that's what you're thinking."

I roll my eyes. "So what did Charlie suggest?"

"Well, she didn't actually suggest it, but she did kinda give me the idea." We come up and stand behind the group and stop. "She told me that you love the show Ghost Adventures. I figured that if you like the show so much, it might be fun to try out the Haunted Walk of Ottawa."

My eyes widen. "Really? I've always wanted to do this!" I jump up, wrapping my arms around his neck and give him a tight squeeze. He hugs me back just as tight.

"Good to hear," he says, setting me back on my feet. "Just remember that when you need someone to hold onto whenever you get scared."

"Pfft," I scoff. "I don't scare easily. Besides, I don't believe in ghosts."

"You don't?"

"Nope. I watch that show for an entirely different reason."

"Oh yeah?" he drawls. "What's that?"

"Zak Bagans."

"Who the fuck is Zak Bagans?"

"He's the host of Ghost Adventures, and he's one of the hottest men alive."

A woman in her early twenties who's standing behind Jase, leans around him and smiles at me. "Damn right," she says. "I've been in love with that man since the very first episode."

I return her smile before I look back to Jase. His eyes move from me to my new friend, and back again before he finally shakes his head. "Zak sounds like a pussy," he declares.

The other woman and I both throw our heads back and laugh, exchanging memories of our favorite episodes of Ghost Adventures. While we talk, Jase quietly takes my hand and listens to the two of us, a smile playing across his lips.

Once the tour starts, we follow along behind everyone, listening to our tour guide tell the different paranormal stories behind some of the larger buildings in the area. Our guide is a young, college-aged guy who can tell a hell of a ghost story, appearing to creep Jase out.

When we reach the final building, Jase is gripping my hand tightly. I've heard horror stories about this place in particular. It's creepy and dark, and the air is significantly colder inside. Serving as a maximum security prison for almost one hundred years, these stone walls contain memories only found in nightmares.

The guide outlines the story for us as we move down the thin, dark corridors. Many areas don't even have windows to allow outside light, and I can't imagine the terror of having to live within these walls when it was an active prison.

He tells us stories of death row inmates and prisoners in solitary confinement, stripped naked and chained to the cold stones inside the cells. Each story makes my heart race, and I can't shake the feeling that we're being watched. Jase seems swept up in the stories too, looking into the cells and commenting on things between the guides' stories.

At one point, the guide opens a large iron door that leads into total blackness, telling us to follow him. He holds his small lantern up in front, and people join a chain as we stumble through the dark narrow hallway, gripping tightly to the back of the person in front of us. Jase is behind me, his hands tight on my shoulders.

"You really like this shit?" he whispers.

"I love it. Best date ever."

"Fuck," he mutters as he shuffles along behind me.

I giggle softly and listen as we approach the gallows of the prison. The guide indicates the large, closed, iron trap doors, and above them hang three nooses. He explains that these very same steps that we stand on are the final steps that over three hundred people had used on their way to be executed.

In the middle of his speech, a large bang rings through the gallows, and several of us scream. The middle noose in the row of three is slowly swinging above a now open trap door.

"That's it," Jase declares. "I'm outta here." He grabs my hand and starts towards the tour guide, dragging me along behind him. I follow willingly, trying not to laugh. "Is this tour almost over?" he asks.

"Yes, sir. This is the final stop. We will be heading to the courtyard now."

"Good," Jase mumbles and I lose it. Laughter bubbles up and I try my best to keep it quiet. "Laugh it up, lady," he says. "That shit is just not natural, and you're one very sick woman if this is the type of stuff you're into."

I laugh all the way outside, and all the way to his bike. Every time I think of his face when he declared that he was done, I laugh even more, and this goes on, all the way back to my house.

Just outside my door, I'm still grinning when Jase laughs. "You're an evil woman, you know that?" Before I can answer, his mouth is on mine, and suddenly I can't even remember what we were talking about.

Jase

I TURN THE wrench one last time and step back to admire my handiwork. This chopper is even more amazing than the last one, and I couldn't be prouder. I just wish that Gunner could have seen the finished product. He'd have liked this one.

With one final glance, I move to the sink and start washing up, getting as much grease as possible out of the calluses on my hands. I need to look good tonight, and that means I can't be looking like a goddamn grease monkey.

I haven't laid eyes on Ellen since our date last Saturday night. We've both been busy with work, and she's had her son to take care of. We've talked on the phone though, every night before she goes to bed. Hearing her sleep laced voice right before I head to bed myself, helps me sleep soundly, but I can only imagine what it would be like to hear that voice next to me every night.

This weekend, I'm hoping to get that chance. Bryce is going to his father's for the first time, for the whole weekend. I know that Ellen is worried, and that she'll be freaking out, but I have nothing but time to help take her mind off that.

"Holy fuck, Jase."

Ryker's voice startles the shit out of me, and I curse myself for going on that damn haunted walk the other night. I've been a jumpy mess ever since, and if I don't calm down soon, I'll have to start shopping in the ladies' department.

I turn and watch as Ryker rounds the chopper, his hand gliding along the chrome reverently. "This is incredible, man. Each one gets better and better."

"Thanks,' I reply, wondering what the hell he's still doing here. Usually on Fridays, he heads home shortly after lunch.

"I wanted to talk to you about something." He looks around at the littered garage floor, taking in the piles of tools organized in milk crates, and the shelves I'd built with scrap wood. My work space is small and cramped, but I do what I can with what I have.

"Now that we've given over our weed business, we're gonna have to find some new, cleaner ways to make some serious profit for this club. We do all right with our strip clubs and night clubs, and of course our garage, but I want more." He waves his hand around the room. "This isn't good enough for you, man. You need more."

I shrug. "It'll do for now."

"But you can't do shit here. Listen, there's a garage for sale just outside the city, about a twenty-minute drive from here. It's been empty for a couple years now, and they're desperate to sell. I put in an offer, and today they accepted it."

I frown. "An offer...for the garage? Why?"

"It's all yours, buddy. Build it up and make it successful. Hire some mechanics and body guys. Sell custom choppers for thousands of dollars. I know Gunner was skeptical, but I have plenty of faith in you."

I stare at him, my eyes wide. "This is crazy! Are you sure? Do you think we can make this work?"

"I think you can," he replies. He turns and walks towards the door. "Anyways, I'll take you by it on Monday, but for now, I'm outta here. Charlie's got the weekend off, told me she has some good news."

I can't believe he's being so casual about this. The man just told me he's gonna make my dream come true, like some kind of messy-haired, tattooed Santa Claus, and now he's off to screw his woman like it's no big deal.

"Ryk," I call, just as he's about to step out of sight.

He takes a step back and looks my way. Taking my fist, I hold it over my heart. "Never forget it, brother."

Several seconds go by before he finally moves, placing his own fist over his heart. He gives me a nod, then he's gone. I look around this pitiful excuse for a garage. Over a month ago, I was pissed that the world didn't seem to want to give me a chance, and now look at me. When the hell did my luck change?

Ellen

My heart's lodged firmly in my throat as I help Bryce pack a bag to take to his father's house. He's running around, talking a mile a minute about all the fun things they have planned for this weekend, totally oblivious to the fact that I'm in the midst of having a nervous breakdown.

"Did you get your toothbrush?"

Bryce rolls his eyes, as he seems to be doing more and more lately. "Yes, Mom. For the third time, I got my toothbrush."

The doorbell rings and Bryce tears off down the hall, yanking the door open. "Dad! I'm just about ready," he says excitedly, throwing his arms around his father's waist.

Paul pats Bryce's head and glares at me from the front step. "Why don't you go grab your stuff," he tells Bryce, never taking his eyes off me.

Bryce passes me in a hurry, almost knocking me over in his rush to get to his bedroom. "They certainly didn't waste any time dipping into my bank account," Paul calls to me.

I have no idea what he's talking about. "Pardon?"

"That money you wanted so bad," he sneers. "The courts have already taken almost half my goddamn paycheck to start paying you."

"I never asked for you for anything, Paul, and certainly not for your money. You took *me* to court, remember? This is not my fault."

"Oh fuck you, Ellen. You've been giving me a hard time since day one. At least now, I can see my fucking kid without having to get a signed permission slip to take him out of your piece of shit house." He takes a step forward, pointing an angry finger in my direction. "I should find a way to make it hard on you now. What do you think of that?"

"What's going on?" I hear from behind me. I spin around, plastering a phony smile on my face.

"Nothing, baby. Just grown-up stuff. You have everything?"

His frown deepens and he looks past me to his father, nodding his head slowly. I can tell by the look on his face that he heard some of what was said, but I can't be sure of how much.

"Let's go!" Paul shouts from the front door. "I don't have all day, Bryce. Get a move on."

Bryce jumps into motion, throwing on his shoes and grabbing his coat from the hook in the closet. "Ready," he calls, and before I know it, he's out the door. I didn't even get a chance to give him a kiss.

I watch through the window as Paul storms to his truck, jumping into the driver's side. Bryce follows along behind him, jumping up as high as he can to reach the handle on the lifted truck. Finally, he gets the door open, throws his bag inside and climbs in. They peel out of the driveway, then they're gone.

I lean against the wall and suddenly everything hits me at once. The court case, Paul's newfound visitation rights, the way Paul talks to me, and Bryce's behaviour…everything. I feel like I'm drowning, and there's nothing I can do to make it go away.

My chest heaves and my throat hurts as I try to keep my crying as calm as possible, when all I really want to do is throw myself on the floor and scream. I hate this all so much, and it feels like it's never going to end. Paul is never going to go away, and he'll never stop being an asshole. Bryce already has a lot of his father's attitude, and now that they'll be spending more time together, that gives Paul even more time to brainwash my son into hating me.

I sit like that for twenty minutes, my knees pulled up to my chest as I let myself have the cry I needed so desperately. The tears help.

Slowly, I feel the tension in my shoulders start to relax, and I think back to the things the judge had said. She was right. Paul is a difficult man, but that doesn't mean that I have to cower every time he comes over. I need to learn to stand up for myself because Paul isn't going away, and no one's going to do it for me.

His passive aggressive comments and threats are never going to stop unless I put a stop to them, and God only knows what he's saying to my son. This is just the first visit in an arrangement of bi-weekly visits for the next seven years. God help me.

Jase

I TAKE THE front steps two at a time and ring Ellen's doorbell with a smile on my face. I can't wait to tell her about the garage and all my plans to make it a success. When the door swings open, I get a look at her face, and my excitement fades.

"Babe, what the hell?" I put my hand to her belly and guide her backwards so that I can come inside, and close the door behind me. "What's wrong?"

She sighs and grasps my wrist, giving it a gentle squeeze. "I'm fine. I just got a little emotional when Paul left with Bryce." I search her eyes, knowing that's not everything.

"What did that prick say to you?" I know he said something. Ellen's tough, and she wouldn't just cry because her son went away for the weekend.

"It's fine, Jase, really. He was no more of an asshole than usual, but I was upset because I realized just how much longer I have to deal with him." She looks away. "And it hurt watching Bryce pack up his stuff in a big hurry to get away from me. I know he doesn't get it, but…" Her shoulders lift in a sad shrug. "Doesn't make it hurt any less."

"He said something else," I push. "I know he did. Tell me." Ellen's teeth sink into her lip and she stares up at me, clearly trying to come to a decision. "Babe," I say, "just tell me."

"He was angry that they took the money from his paycheck for child support. He was acting like I asked for the money, even though it was him that took me to court in the first place. He was blaming me, saying I just wanted to make things hard on him." She takes a deep breath and looks off to the side. "He said that maybe he needs to find a way to make things hard for me."

I grit my teeth and try to fight back the anger that washes over me. That son of a bitch had never had any part in this kid's life until a year ago, and now he's frustrated that he has to pay? Fucking deadbeat. My father may not have won the father of the year award, but he always made sure I was taken care of, and that I had what I needed. It sounds like the time has come for me to finally meet this fucker, and help him to understand a few things.

I pull her into my arms, wishing that I could make this whole thing go away for her. She wraps her arms around me and takes a deep breath, her body tense.

"Wanna get out of here?" I suggest.

"Not really," she says, scrubbing her hands down her face. "I'd rather just sit here and feel sorry for myself with a tub of Ben & Jerry's, to be honest."

"Nope," I say. "Not happenin'. Get your purse, woman. We're going out."

She complains a bit, but with a little more coaxing, she heads to the bathroom and freshens up.

Outside, I hand her the helmet that I now think of as hers, and wait while she does up the strap. "Where to?" she asks as she climbs on behind me.

"There's a party at he clubhouse tonight. I wasn't gonna go, but I think you and I could both use a beer. Besides, you haven't been there yet, have you?"

She shakes her head and I grin, starting up the motorcycle. I take the long way, feeling the tension leave Ellen's body the longer I drive. One thing that a lot of people don't get is that riding a Harley isn't just a mode of transportation. It's fucking therapy. No matter how pissed off I get, or how worried I am about something, hopping on my bike and going for a ride makes me feel better every single time.

We pull into the compound and I wait while she climbs off, my eyes scanning the long line of motorcycles, trying to figure out who's here. I'm surprised when I see Ryker's ride standing proudly at the front of the line. I thought he said he had plans with Charlie.

Taking Ellen's hand, I head inside, weaving through the large crowd of people gathered. Every Friday night is busy at the Kings' clubhouse, but tonight is busier than usual. Bosco's leaning against the wall in a relatively empty part of the room.

"Hey, Bos. What's with all the civies?"

Bosco chuckles. "Fuckin' bunch of fools were at the Pig's Ear and got into a fight." He waves his hand, indicating the far side of the room where two patched members, Hulk and HaHa sit, surrounded by a group of women I've never seen before. "They invited a bunch of the ladies back here after the bouncer kicked their asses out."

Great. We're not forbidden from having outsiders coming into the clubhouse, but having a bunch of them here at once never goes well, and always ends in some idiot civie getting his or her ass kicked. I look to the left to see Lucy and a couple of the other whores scowling at them all, clearly not happy to have their territory invaded. There is no way this is going to end well.

As the new VP, it's probably my duty to do something about this before shit gets out of hand, but I decide to let it go for now. I have something to celebrate, and Ellen needs to get her mind off her problems. Besides, how much trouble can a few women get into anyways?

Grabbing her hand, we move to the back of the room where Ryker and Charlie are sitting at a tall table with Tease and Laynie. "Hey fuckers," I tease, pulling out one of the bar stools for Ellen. "Ryk, I thought you said you and Charlie were gonna be doing shit together, away from here this weekend."

"Yeah, but it turns out Charlie had a surprise for me when I got home. I was hoping you'd show up here because you're the first one I wanted to know."

"Oh my God," Laynie squeals at the same time Ellen asks, "You are?"

Charlie grins at the two ladies and nods her head excitedly. "I'm pregnant." All three women let out an ear-piercing screech that draws the attention of everyone in the room.

"Did you hear that everyone?" I yell. "Ryk's gonna be a daddy!"

Rounds of cheering fill the room, and people start shuffling forward with beers, offering the happy couple their congratulations. I've never seen Charlie smile so big as she does when she talks about how she found out she was pregnant, and I watch my best friend as he smiles at his wife when she tells the story. He doesn't take his eyes off of her.

I take Ellen's hand and give it a squeeze.

"You were right," she shouts over the drone of loud and drunken conversation. "This was exactly what I needed."

"Oh!" Charlie shouts, almost jumping out of her chair. "Did you tell Ellen *your* good news?"

Ellen turns to me. "You have good news?"

"I was going to tell you later, but now's as good a time as any. Ryker and the rest of the Kings are gonna give me a hand opening up my own garage. Ryker's already found me a building."

"What?" she says, throwing her arms around my neck. "That's awesome, Jase! I know how important that is to you."

I can't hide my smile. Deciding that we need something more than beer to celebrate, I get up and make my way to the bar, searching for a fresh bottle of Patrón. I kneel down and look on the shelves underneath, shoving aside half-open bottles until I finally find what I'm looking for.

Standing with my prize in hand, I meet a familiar pair of blue eyes that I never thought I'd see again.

"Jase," she smiles. "I was hoping I'd see you here."

My body freezes. "Tawney, what are you doing here?"

Ellen

"How far along do you think you are?"

Charlie looks at me and beams, her smile lighting up the entire dreary room. "About six weeks, I think. I go for an ultrasound on Friday to see for sure."

"That's great news," I gush. I had no idea that this was something that Charlie and Ryker were wanting, but looking at them now, there's no doubt that they're ecstatic about the news.

Her eyes go beyond me, and I watch them narrow, anger flashing across her previously happy face. Turning, I follow her gaze and see Jase leaning against the bar, talking to a blonde woman, a smile on his face. A slow burn starts in my stomach as I watch her touch his arm, throwing her head back in laughter over something he says. I can't see her face, but I can tell from here that she has a very attractive body, and isn't afraid to show it off.

"Uh, Ryk," Tease says, interrupting my moment of shameless spying. "We might have a problem."

I follow the path his finger is pointing and see a group of three women charging towards Jase and the woman he's talking to.

"Shit!" Ryker spits as he jumps out of his seat, hurrying to intercept the women.

"What's going on?"

"The club whores aren't liking all the new ladies walking around here tonight, and they're about to make a move to protect what's theirs," Tease drawls.

I watch as the women start screaming over Ryker's shoulder, calling the other woman some nasty names that I've never even heard before.

"What's theirs?" I ask, my stomach sinking as I turn back to watch the show. "Is Jase theirs?"

"They think so," he replies as he gets up to help Ryker and Jase keep the screaming women apart. Just as he reaches the group, I watch as the mystery woman turns and charges at the others, and I finally get a look at her face.

It's Tawney, the woman from the bar that had given Jase a blow-job in the bathroom. Bile works its way up my throat, and I suddenly feel like I can't breathe. Jase snakes his arm around Tawney's waist and pulls her back against him, yelling for everyone to calm down.

I can't watch this anymore. I feel numb as I stand from my seat and head for the exit. I vaguely hear Charlie calling my name, but I feel like my head is spinning. I push my way through the cheering crowd as they jeer the women on, anxious for a fight to break out. Finally, after what feels like forever, I make it outside.

I step out into the night air and breathe deeply. The air is starting to get cooler, and I know that our long summer is coming to an end. Wrapping my arms around myself, I turn the corner and press my back against the cold brick. The noise from inside still reaches me, but I can no longer make out the words, and I don't want to. I don't want to hear them screaming about who owns who, and who needs to get the fuck out.

Inside, my mind is racing. What was Tawney doing here? And why did Jase seem to be so friendly with her after what had gone on between them? I think the part that bothers me the most is why do the club whores think that Jase belongs to *them*? Is he still sleeping with them? Thinking about it makes me want to puke.

"Jesus, El. You scared the hell out of me. What are you doing out here, hiding in the dark?"

I roll my eyes. "I didn't think you'd notice. You seemed to have your hands pretty full in there."

He chuckles. "What, those bitches? I don't give a fuck about them."

"That's the problem!" I yell, frustration taking me so high that I can't find my way back down. "You don't care about them. You use them, and you think this thing between us is just one big fucking joke. But it isn't a joke to me, Jase. I can't deal with this shit. I can't deal with your life, or your past, or any of the hundreds of women that come along with it!" I push off from the wall and hold my hands out in defeat. "I have a little boy to take care of. I can't do this."

I go to step around him, just wanting to get the hell out of here, when he steps in front of me, blocking my escape. "When are you going to quit fuckin' hiding behind your kid, El?"

I jerk my head back as if I've been slapped. "I don't hide behind Bryce."

"Bullshit!" he yells. "Since the very first time I asked you out, you've spouted off your bullshit about all the stuff going on in your life, but the truth is, you've been hiding—hiding from life, hiding from me, and hiding from ever taking a risk with your heart again."

"I do—"

"You do! No matter how hard I try, you always find a way to shove me back, and every fuckin' time, you use him as an excuse."

"Well I don't trust you!" I blurt.

"And there it is," Jase says. "The real reason you run scared all the time.

"Your history speaks for itself!"

"And you don't believe people can change?"

"I don't want to be on the losing end of taking that chance."

"Are you into me?"

"I…what does—"

"Just answer the fuckin' question. Are you into me?" he screams, his face twisted in anger.

"Yes," I scream back.

Jase's body hits mine before I can blink, backing me up against the wall. His lips are all over mine, his tongue sliding inside my mouth. It's like a switch gets flipped in my brain, and suddenly, all thoughts of Paul, Bryce, and my fight with Jase, leave my mind, and all I can think about is how much I need this man inside of me. I kiss him back, my body trembling with need.

Jase pulls back and glares down at me. "Can you do this? Can you handle this?"

"Shut up," I breathe, reaching for his face once more. His lips claim mine in another hot, hungry kiss. Snaking my hands up under his shirt, I run my fingers up his muscled abs.

His lips go to my ear and he pants heavily when he says, "I need to be inside you, El."

"God, I need that too," I admit. I shoot my hands out, reaching for his belt buckle, desperate to get him out of his pants. Jase grabs my wrists, mumbling something about going upstairs, but I don't listen. "Four years, Jase," I cry as I yank his pants down over his hips.

His chuckle of amusement turns to a hiss as I grip his cock in my hands, marvelling at the size, wondering just how I'm going to accommodate that from a standing position. Jase curses and grabs for my jeans, yanking them down my legs until they hit my knees. Before I know it, he's spun me around and has my chest pressed against the wall.

My breathing comes out in sharp bursts as I stand there, my legs held together at the knees by my jeans, listening to Jase fumble with a condom wrapper. "Next time will be better, baby. I promise."

"Just fuck me, Jase. Please."

Jase grabs my hips and pulls them towards him, so I'm bent at the waist, my hands pressed against the brick. I feel his cock at my entrance, and then slowly, he fills me. He groans loudly when he gets all the way inside, and I moan.

He starts to move in and out, picking up speed with each thrust, and I can already feel my orgasm building. I don't know if it's the angle, or the fact that it's Jase, but I do know that sex has never felt this good.

"Fuck, baby. This isn't going to last long." His thrusts get wilder and out of control. The brick bites into my palms as my pleasure builds. "Fuck, Ellen," Jase gasps.

My climax washes over me and rolls through my body, my pussy clamping tight on Jase's cock. His fingers dig into my hips, just as I feel him swell inside me, his own climax taking over.

We stay in that position for a few seconds, both of us trying to catch our breaths.

Jase slowly pulls out and spins me around, righting my pants and placing a tender kiss on the palm of my hands. I smile up at him and his face is full of emotion as he lowers his lips to mine. Slowly, he kisses me, making me feel more special to him than I've ever felt to anyone in my life.

He pulls away and grins, reaching down to pull up his own jeans and lets out a startled yelp. "Jesus Christ!"

I look and see Dexter, Laynie's dog, standing by the corner, watching us with his tongue hanging out.

Just then, a figure steps out of the shadows about twenty feet away, hurrying towards the door. "Sorry," Laynie mumbles. "I was just taking the dog out and...well, I didn't see anything, so there's that. On the other hand, my ears work fine, so I'm off to go see if Tease can bleach my ear drums for me." With that parting note, she whistles for Dexter and disappears back inside the clubhouse.

"Oh God!" I cry. "What must she think of me?"

Jase laughs. "Please. If I know Laynie, she's in there begging Tease to bring her out here and do the same damn thing. Don't worry about it, babe. Really."

He pulls me into his arms and kisses the top of my head. "Are we okay?"

I sigh. "Why were you flirting with her while I was sitting there?"

"Honestly, I was apologizing. I told her I was sorry, and that I was a real dick. I told her I'd met an amazing woman that made me realize that, and I wanted to set the record straight with her."

"And the other girls?"

"I don't control what they do. Lucy and the girls, they work to keep their place in this clubhouse. They don't like competition."

"So does that mean I'm competition?"

He nods. "Absolutely." I stare at him with wide eyes. "To them you are. You just have to stake your claim, babe. They'll get the hint."

I remember the stories Charlie had told me about Lucy, and how she'd tried to push Charlie around in the beginning. Charlie had dealt with her, sort of. It was Laynie who finally put Lucy in her place by punching her in the face. God, I hope I don't have to punch anybody in the face.

"Let's not worry about that tonight, okay? Look, I have an idea."

"What's that?" All I can think about is the whorehouse show-down that I might need to participate in if I want to keep those bitches away from my man.

"Well," he drawls, swiping his thumb across my lip and wagging his eyebrows. "I happen to know of a little house in the city that's completely empty right now."

Jase

I WAKE UP to the scent of vanilla tickling my nostrils and a warm body wrapped tightly around my torso. I'm surrounded by peace and quiet, the only sounds coming from a ticking clock, somewhere in the house.

For the first time I can remember, I've gotten a full night's sleep, and am not woken up in the morning by women screaming at someone in another room, or men fighting about who stole the last beer. The clubhouse is noisy and full of people all the time. It's all I've ever known, but this—this quiet house with Ellen—I could get used to.

I slide my hand up her bare arm and squeeze her gently, burying my nose in her hair. She draws a deep breath in through her nose, her entire body straightening as she slowly stretches out her limbs. Letting her arms go loose around my waist, her big brown eyes open and stare into mine, a wide grin on her perfect lips.

"Morning."

"Good morning."

"How'd you sleep?"

"Like a rock. Don't know if it was the bed or the girl, but I slept better than I have in years."

She smiles. "Good." Resting her head back on my chest, she traces lightly up and down my skin with the tips of her fingers, causing goose bumps to race along behind them. My heart hammers inside my chest, my breathing laboured.

Reaching for her, I tip her head back and slide my lips against hers. "Last night with you was incredible, baby, but today, I'm gonna take my time with you. You deserve more than just a quick fuck against the wall, El. You deserve to be honored, loved, and worshipped." I press a my lips to hers. "Let me worship you, baby."

Moving my body, I keep my lips on her and roll her to her back, my tongue taking advantage of her gasp and finding its way inside. I press myself against her side and deepen our kiss, turning my head as I slide my tongue across hers, reveling in the way she tastes.

My fingertips find the hem of her tiny tank top and I slip them inside, gliding my palm up her smooth belly until my hand meets the underside of her breast. Cupping it gently, I swipe my tongue across her lips and pull back, staring into her eyes as I roll her nipple gently between my thumb and forefinger.

She stares back at me with hooded eyes, her teeth sunk into her lower lip. I roll it again, and smile when she moans. The next time I roll the tight little bud, I give it a pinch and watch with fascination as her eyes fall closed. My girl likes a little pain mixed with her pleasure. This is good news.

I reach for her shirt and peel it from her body, tossing it behind me to land somewhere on the floor. I pull back and stare down at her body, taking it in for the first time, the morning sun shining off her skin. She's gorgeous, and I want to see all of her. That tiny strip of fabric she calls panties are blocking my view. Reaching forward, I slip my fingers in the sides and slide them down her legs, not missing the flash of her pussy as she lifts them to assist me.

My cock is throbbing and screaming at me to hurry this up, always ready to jump inside any pussy it can find, but this time is different. Ellen is different. I'm gonna show her just how good things with me can be.

Stretching out beside her, I claim her mouth again and run my hand up the outside of her thigh, amazed at how smooth her skin is. When I reach her hip, I slide it across to her belly button and back down again, my fingers finding her trimmed patch of hair just below.

I give it a gentle tug and swallow down her gasp, then lower my fingers, finding her wet and ready. "Fuck, baby, you're so wet."

She nods, her lips and teeth biting at mine. Her hips start to sway, trying to make more contact with my hand. I watch her hips thrust at nothing, leaving my finger just above her clit so that it barely touches it.

"Touch me."

I roll the pad of my finger in a circle around her clit. "Like this?"

She whimpers, and I pull my hand away. "Don't tease me, Jase Matthews. Don't you dare tease me."

I fight back a smile. "I won't tease you, baby." Sliding my body down, I settle myself between her legs and stare up at her wide eyes. Slowly, I run my tongue up her slit, parting her lips as I go. When I reach her clit, she jumps and winds her fingers through my hair, cursing as she presses herself against my face.

I love eating pussy. If it was a professional sport, I'd hold the world record. But I've never enjoyed eating pussy more than I enjoy Ellen's. She tastes clean and sweet. Her hips sway with abandon while I nip, lick, and suck at her clit.

Her strangled moan echoes throughout the quiet house as I lap at her with my tongue, drawing out her pleasure for as long as I can. When her body stops trembling, I climb up her body and settle myself between her legs.

My eyes widen in shock when I hear the ripping of the condom wrapper. "Where did you get that?"

"Doesn't matter," she says. "Now roll over."

I do as I'm told, curious to see what this little minx has in mind. My back barely hits the mattress before she swings a leg over top of me. I watch as she carefully rolls on the condom and settles herself over my aching cock.

She lowers herself onto me, and my hands automatically go to her hips. Staring into my eyes, she positions herself in a way that I know the base of my cock is rubbing against her already sensitive clit. I watch, my breathing choppy and shallow, as her tits bounce and her body flushes from exertion.

When her body starts to tremble, and I feel her pussy start to pulse, I switch positions, getting to my knees and sitting back on my calves as she continues to ride me. Her hands are everywhere, and I can't watch her face come undone when she's moving. Grabbing her wrists, I hold them gently, but firmly, behind her back, and drive myself inside her.

Her heavy breathing eventually turns to shouts and curses. Finally, with a deep, hard thrust, she screams my name as her body shatters with her release, and I feel my own building low in my spine.

It's not until her hooded eyes meet mine that I finally follow her over the edge. My sweat slicked skin slides against hers as I lay her back down on the bed and fall down beside her. The two of us lie side by side, our fingers tangled together as we pull ourselves back together.

"Jase? I..." I look down at her, my eyes studying hers as she seems to be having some sort of internal struggle. "I was wondering if you were hungry."

I cock my head and watch her for a moment, wondering what she was really going to say, but decide to drop it for now. "I could eat."

She places a kiss on my lips before crawling from the bed and slipping into my T-shirt. "Pancakes sound good?"

Ellen

"Mom." Bryce calls from the front door. "I'm home."

My eyes land on Jase and my nervous butterflies go crazy. Maybe this isn't a good idea. After spending the entire weekend together, lounging in bed, making love, and watching countless scary movies, Jase had told me that he thought it would be a good idea for him to be here when Paul dropped Bryce off. I'd been worried that it would just make things worse, but Jase asked me trust him, spouting off something about guy codes and messages. Something I don't understand, but Jase assured me Paul would.

"Relax," he whispers, standing from the couch. "It'll be fine." He pulls me to my feet and motions for me to go ahead of him. I move towards the front door, Jase right on my heels.

Paul and Bryce are standing just inside the door, Paul watching Bryce take off his shoes. Both of their heads whip up when we enter the front hall. "Hey, Bud," I say with the brightest smile I can manage. "Did you have a good time with your dad?"

Bryce shrugs and looks over my shoulder. "What's he doing here?" he asks.

Jase squeezes my shoulder in a silent show of support that I couldn't be more grateful for. I can feel Paul's angry eyes boring into me, but I keep my focus on Bryce and smile. "Jase is staying for dinner."

Bryce shrugs again and turns to his dad, ready to say goodbye, but Paul isn't paying any attention to his son. I watch as Bryce's shoulders droop and he looks down at the floor, his face sad and defeated.

"I don't believe we've met," Paul states, holding his hand out to Jase, his jaw set in a hard line. "Paul Chapman."

Jase leans around me, grasping Paul's hand and giving it a single pump. "Jase Matthews," he says formally, and I can't help but grin at the look on Paul's face. If I know Jase, he's squeezing the shit out of Paul's hand right now.

He finally releases him, and I watch as Paul opens and closes his hand, his features frozen in anger. "Ellen, can I talk to you alone please?" He words it like a question, but he isn't asking. His tone is clear.

My mind races for an excuse, but Jase beats me to the punch. "Actually, Paul, that won't be necessary."

"What?" Paul asks, like he can't believe what he's hearing.

"Bryce," I rush out. "Why don't you take your stuff to your room, okay?"

Bryce looks from me to his father, and then to Jase, a deep frown creasing his brow. But thankfully, he doesn't argue as he grabs his backpack and walks to his room. We all watch him go, and then Jase picks up where we left off.

"I said no, Paul. No. You won't be talking to Ellen alone. From what I understand, you're kind of an asshole to her, and she doesn't feel comfortable with you."

Paul gapes at me. "Who the fuck is this guy, Ellen?"

"This guy," Jase continues, "is her man. And this guy doesn't like how things have been going between you two lately, so he intends to be around to make sure things change, for everyone."

Paul's face flushes with anger, a little vein on his left temple threatening to burst. "I thought it was agreed on in court that you would stay away from this son of a bitch."

I smirk and prop my hands on my hips, my back leaning against Jase for support. "You were wrong. It was brought up, but I never agreed to anything."

Paul curses and glares back at both of us, then turns and slams his way out the door, every window in the house shaking from the force.

Bryce comes rushing out of his room, his face ashen as he looks around Jase and I. "Where's Dad?"

The look on his face nearly breaks me. Damn Paul for making him crave his affection so much, and damn him straight to hell for never fully giving it to him. "He went home, Buddy, but he said to say goodbye, and that he'd see you in a couple of weeks."

Bryce's lips press into a thin line and he shakes his head, turning to go back to his room. "Hey, Bryce," Jase calls. "Your mother was just about to start supper. I was thinking you could show me how to play some of those video games I saw in the living room."

Bryce stares up at Jase. "Whatever." He wanders into the living room, calling back behind him, "What game?"

Jase

RIDING ALONG BEHIND Ryker. I finally feel like my life is starting to fall into place. I'm VP of a club that I would lay down my life to protect. My best friend is taking huge steps to show me that he doesn't think of me as a joke, helping to make my dream a reality. I'm building a relationship with a hilarious kid that's turning out to be one of the coolest people I know, and I have a gorgeous, kind, funny woman that I'm starting to wonder how I ever lived without.

The garage itself is just outside of town, a short stretch down a country road. The idea of driving to work every day is new for me. I've only ever had to haul my ass out of bed and drag it across the parking lot to the garage at the compound. This, though, I could get used to.

We come to the top of a hill and just up ahead, I see it. The garage is large, and in need of a paint job, but that's all cosmetic. As we draw closer, I count six separate bay doors, and what looks to be a large customer service area.

Pulling into the driveway, we pull our bikes into a line with

Ryker at the head. Reaper, Tease, and a couple of the other guys came along, wanting to check the place out as well. We all climb off our bikes and look around. As I do, all I can see is potential. This place is fucking perfect.

"Catch," Ryker calls. I turn just in time to catch the keys he tosses at me. "Go check it out."

I grin back at him and move to the door, turning the lock and pushing inside. The customer service area is filthy, and the counter is falling apart. The linoleum is faded and ripped in several places. There are bright rectangles and squares on the wall where the paint is brighter from being covered with posters.

Pushing through the door towards the garages, the guys follow me, all of them making comments about the work that needs to be done. I pay no attention to them and take in my surroundings. Each bay is connected and wide open, with no walls separating them. There are steel shelves lining the back wall, and auto lifts located in front of all six doors. The place is bright from the many windows that reside high up on the cement walls.

"What do you think?" Ryker asks. "This is the first I've really checked out the inside. I didn't realize it needed so much work."

"Are you kidding? That's the best part. It means I can make it exactly the way I want it. This place is fuckin' incredible, Ryk."

"You ladies want us to leave so you can make out?" Reaper drawls. Ryker and I both turn without a word, giving him our middle fingers.

I walk back into the customer service area. "No, seriously. Think about it. This wall is all windows. We can replace the panes with one solid piece of glass. We can rip out the service desk and put a smaller one over there. New paint, new tile, and rip out the little waiting area. This whole room will become a gorgeous fucking showroom to show off some of our best choppers."

We spend the next hour wandering around, making plans and suggestions for all the changes that need to be made. The garage itself is pretty much perfect and ready to use. As soon as Reaper finishes taking inventory of everything he needs to build me a kick-ass security system, we lock up and return to our bikes.

"So what are you gonna name it?" Tease asks as he climbs onto his bike.

"I have no idea."

Ellen

I unlock the door to my house and glare at Bryce as he hurries inside, heading straight for his bedroom. I grit my teeth, ignoring the urge to go down there and rip a strip off him for the shit he pulled today.

Shortly after one o'clock this afternoon, I'd received a phone call from the school asking me to come in right away. Since I was at work, I had to get someone to come in early to cover the rest of my shift, then take the twenty-minute bus ride to the school. By the time I got there, school was getting out for the day.

I'd walked down the hall and found Bryce sitting in the office, looking worried. I didn't even get a chance to talk to him before the principal had pulled us into her office, where she informed me that Bryce had been caught fighting with another boy. The other kids that had witnessed the fight all confirmed that Bryce was the instigator. I'd looked at my son and been shocked by the angry and distant look in his eyes as he refused to tell me what had happened.

Thankfully, the principal had been gracious, letting Bryce off with a warning, but part of that warning was that next time Bryce got caught fighting at school, he would be suspended for three days, without question.

The entire way home, I'd tried to talk to him and find out what had gone down, but he kept saying that I wouldn't understand. By the time we got here, I'd reached my limit in patience. I check my watch and realize that it's later than I thought, and that Jase will be here any minute.

This is the second night this week that Jase has been over for supper, and to get to know Bryce a little better. Bryce is still unsure about the whole thing, but I think he's slowly coming around. Jase has been extremely understanding of Bryce, and how our relationship affects him, never pushing himself on either one of us.

I move to the kitchen and begin preparing dinner, trying to come up with some sort of solution on how to deal with my son. I'm at a loss. As a mother, I feel like a failure—like there's something I should be doing to fix this for him, but I have no idea what that something is.

The doorbell rings and I hurry down the hall, wiping my fingers on a dish towel. I swing the door open and when my eyes land on Jase, all the tension in my body fades. His perfect smile hits me, and I practically throw myself at him, wrapping my arms around his neck.

"Hey, what's wrong?"

I pull away, motioning for him to come in. We move into the kitchen where I grab him a beer and go back to cutting potatoes while I tell him what had happened today. "I don't even know what to say to him right now. It's like everything I do say pisses him off even more, and sometimes it even feels like he hates me."

Tears form in my eyes as I think about what the hell I'm supposed to do about this whole mess. Jase's smile is gone.

"I'm sorry," I say, moving towards him and collapsing against him. "You don't want to hear about this."

"Yes, I do," he states matter of factly, pressing a kiss to the top of my head. "I was just thinking. I hate seeing you so upset about this, and I hate that something is going on with Bryce."

"Thank you."

He places his arms on my elbows and holds me away from him. "Do you think it would be okay if I talked to him?"

"Honestly, I don't know if that's such a good idea. I mean, you barely know Bryce, and he's not exactly the nicest kid lately."

"Look, I won't talk to him if you don't want me to, but maybe it would help if he had a man to talk to." I study his face, my mind racing over all the possible outcomes of this little talk. He holds his hands out in surrender. "I promise, I won't push him. I'll just test the waters."

"Fine," I relent, deciding that it's worth a shot.

I follow Jase down the hall to Bryce's room. He knocks and waits for Bryce to answer, giving me a wink just before he steps inside. He knows I'm going to listen. From my place in the hall, I can't see them, but I can hear them clearly.

"Hey, B. Your mom said you had a rough day."

"So?"

"So, I came to see if you wanted to talk."

"Why would I want to talk to you?"

"Because I'm a good listener and because I'd like to help you make things better." I have to give him credit. Jase is already displaying much more patience than me at this point.

"What do you care? You're not my dad."

Jase laughs. "Yeah, I'm definitely not. Listen, about your fight—"

"That kid's an asshole. He was making these annoying sounds, and I told him to shut up, but he wouldn't listen."

"So you made him shut up." Silence fills the air. "If that's the case, B, I hate to say it, but it sounds like you're the asshole."

"What?"

"You bullied that kid because he wasn't doing what you wanted him to do. That's the definition of an asshole."

"My dad called me a pussy," he mumbles, so low I can barely hear him. "I wanted to prove that I wasn't." My heart clenches. Is Paul still talking to my kid like this?

"So you were trying to be a badass?" I wait for Bryce's answer, but don't hear anything before Jase continues. "Well, I'm gonna let you in on a little secret, okay? You don't have to be an asshole to be a badass. You just have to be someone who believes in himself, and not the bullshit that other people put in your head."

"Do you really think I'm an asshole, Jase?"

Jase sighs. "No, kid, I don't. I just think you need to find your inner badass."

Bryce mumbles something I can't hear, but I do hear Jase moving towards the door. "I'm gonna go help your mom with supper. You think about that, yeah?"

"Yeah. Thanks, Jase."

"Anytime, little man. I'm always around."

When Jase steps into the hall, I watch as he approaches. His seems unsure, probably because he knows I don't approve of his language choices. It's bad enough to hear the words that come out of Bryce's mouth these days.

When he gets close enough, I whisper, "Thank you."

Twenty-One

Jase

"CAN I SEE THE inside?" Bryce asks. climbing down from the back of my bike. It had taken a lot of convincing from both me and Bryce to get Ellen to allow this little excursion. but after more than a week of Bryce begging, she'd finally agreed.

"Sure can." I walk up to the door and unlock it, swinging it wide open so Bryce can go running in.

The second he gets inside. he stops, curling his lip in disgust. "What a dump."

"Hey, B?"

Bryce wanders around, looking the place over. "Yeah?"

"You need to learn to think it, not say it."

His cheeks flush and he grins. "Sorry, Jase. but it is."

"It's not a dump. It just needs a bit of a facelift. You watch, this place is gonna be the coolest garage around. and you can help."

"Really?"

I laugh at the eagerness I hear in his voice. "Yes sir. I've got a paint roller with your name all over it."

Bryce rolls his eyes. "Great."

My phone chimes with a text, and I pull my phone out to see that it's from Ellen.

Ellen: My kid driving you crazy yet?

I look up and watch as Bryce peers into the cavernous garage beyond the door. "Cool," he whispers and steps inside. I smile to myself and text her back.

Me: We're cool, woman. Stop worrying.

Things have been good between the three of us since Bryce's little incident at school last week. I'd been over just about every night, visiting with Ellen and hanging out with Bryce. In that time, I'd gotten to know him a little better, and he's a cool kid. He's got a mouth on him, but in a way, that's kind of my favorite thing about him. It reminds me of me at that age. He just needs to learn when it's not okay to be mouthy, particularly when he's talking to his mother.

I know that Ellen is starting to get nervous because tomorrow Paul will be coming to pick up Bryce again for their weekend visit. After finding out how he talks to her son, she's not looking forward to sending him back there, and I have to say I'm not either, but she has a court order, and she insists on following it.

I stuff my phone back into my pocket and step into the garage, flipping on the lights by the door. "What do ya think?"

"This is cool."

"Yeah?" I ask, unable to hide my grin.

"Definitely! We could have an entire basketball game in here! It's huge." He looks around the room. "What are you gonna call it?"

"I haven't quite thought of that yet."

"What about something simple, like King's Garage?"

"Too simple."

"Kings of Korruption Custom Choppers?"

"Too long."

"I know!" He grins wide. "Korrupted Custom Choppers!"

I mull the name over in my mind. Simple, but shows that it's a club business. "I like it. Not too boring, and still sounds cool."

Bryce's grin widens and his chest puffs out just a little. "Awesome."

"We should head back before your mom has a heart attack, picturing you lyin' in a ditch somewhere."

Bryce rolls his eyes and lumbers towards the door, clearly not happy to be leaving. I like the fact that he wants to be here. If he likes it, I'll bring him here as often as he wants. Maybe I can even pass along some of the mechanical stuff my father taught me.

After locking up, I place the helmet on Bryce's head and go to climb on the bike. "Jase?"

I take in Bryce's suddenly sullen form, his eyes on the pavement in front of him, alarmed by the sudden shift in mood. "What's up?"

"I need to tell you something. I was gonna tell Mom, but I know she'll freak out, and well…you kinda calm her down when she starts to freak, so I thought maybe I could tell you, and then you could tell her, and—"

"B, slow down. You can tell me anything. What is it?"

Bryce bites his lip and looks up at me from under his giant helmet, his eyes full of uncertainty. "I don't want to go with my dad tomorrow."

I kneel down in front of him, the pavement biting into my knee as I place my hands on his shoulders. "Then you won't go. Your mom doesn't want you to go either."

Hope fills his features. "Really?"

"Really. She hates it. But I need to ask, why don't you wanna go with him all of a sudden?"

"He's just mean, and he was never mean before."

My body tenses. If that fucker's laid a hand on this kid, I will rip him apart. "Did he hurt you, B?"

He shakes his head. "No, he never touched me. He mostly ignored me, and when he did talk to me, he called me names and said bad stuff about Mom. I just don't want to go back there."

Drawing in slow and steady breaths, I do my best to hide my rage, but right now, I want nothing more than to find that son of a bitch and make him bleed. I stand from my place on the ground and squeeze Bryce's shoulder. "He won't get that chance again, B. I promise you that."

Bryce nods, and I can see his tiny body tremble. He tries so hard to be tough all the time, but this kid has his own share of demons thanks to that prick, and no matter what Ellen does, and me, if I'm lucky, we won't be able to take those away. I just hope we can teach him to quiet them.

"Let's go home. Supper must be ready."

"One more thing," he blurts.

Shit. I don't know if I can hear much more. I already want to murder the stupid fuck. I don't know how much more I can take.

"I have a basketball game on Monday, and Mom can't go. Do you think you could come, and maybe watch me play?"

"You kiddin' me? You don't even have to ask, kid. I'll be there."

Bryce's grin makes the anger fade, just a little. He climbs on behind me and we head for home. I spend the entire drive plotting out exactly how this is gonna go down with Paul.

Ellen

I make it to the coffee shop a little later than expected. The bus was running fifteen minutes behind, causing me to miss my transfer bus. This is just not my day. I'd slept in this morning, spilled my coffee all over the kitchen table, and stabbed myself in the eyeball with my mascara wand, not once, but twice. I'm ready for it to be over.

Seeing Charlie and Laynie at a table on the patio, I get my coffee and danish and move outside to join them. "Hey!" Charlie says as I approach. "We were worried you weren't going to make it."

I smile and take a seat before turning my attention to Charlie. "So, did you have your ultrasound?"

Her face breaks out into a wide smile. "I did. I'm due May third. That makes me eight weeks tomorrow."

The three of us squeal like a bunch of school girls. We spend the next hour talking about babies, and thinking up unique baby names that I sincerely hope she never actually considers.

"So," Laynie prompts, changing the subject. "How are things

with Jase?"

My face heats and I sputter a little as I think back to what she heard that night. "Good," I choke out. "Great."

Laynie's head falls back and laughter bursts from her small frame. "What's going on?" Charlie asks.

"I'll let Ellen tell you," Laynie manages to say between bursts of giggles.

"That night at the clubhouse, when you told us all about the baby, Jase and I got into a bit of a fight, as you know." Laynie sputters and giggles some more. Charlie frowns and cocks her head at her clearly insane friend, motioning for me to continue.

"Anyways, we ended up making up..." Laynie snorts and I continue, "Against the wall, around the side of the clubhouse. Laynie was outside with Dex and heard it all."

"Oh God," Charlie says, trying hard to sound serious, but I don't miss the laughter in here voice. "That's hilarious." The three of us burst into a wild round of laughter.

Once we've all settled down and are starting to catch our breaths, Charlie speaks again. "So, did you get it worked out?"

"What?"

"Whatever it was you were fighting about? It was that girl, wasn't it? The one from the bar that night."

I nod. "We worked it out. We're good now, actually. He's been coming over a lot, and even spending some quality time with my son, so that's good. Different for all of us, but good." I polish off the rest of my coffee and place my cup back on the table. "Can I ask you ladies something?"

They both nod.

"Is being an old lady hard?" I ask.

Laynie is the first to speak. "It's got its moments. Your man can't tell you everything all the time. Sometimes, he has to do things that go against everyone's moral code, including his own, and that's not fun. Sometimes, they do things that are dangerous, but you may never even know about."

"On the other hand," Charlie continues, "you will never find a man as fierce and loyal, more loving, or more protective than these men. They love their ladies, and they love them hard."

"What about the whores?" I blurt out. It's why I asked in the first place.

"They're just that—whores. They're there to keep the men happy, and are all hoping to land the title of old lady someday."

"And you're okay with that? With them keeping your man happy?" Maybe I can't handle this as well as I thought.

Charlie laughs. "God, no. When Ryker and I first got together, they tried to get rid of me. One of them gave it her best shot, but I ignored her and held on tight. Besides, I find creative ways of my own to keep him happy."

We all laugh, getting disapproving looks from the old lady a few tables over. "That girl, the one that tried to get rid of you, you ignored her?"

Laynie raises her hand. "*I* didn't ignore her. That bitch gave me a hard time too. I broke her nose."

"I don't know if I can do that."

"You won't have to."

Charlie's phone alerts her of a text, and we all wait while she checks it. Her hand covers her mouth and she sits up straight in her chair. "Oh my God," she says breathlessly. "Sarah's in labour!"

"She is!" Laynie cries, reaching for her purse.

"Yes! Ryker just texted me. He said she texted Bosco, looking for a ride. He's staying with her until you get there."

Laynie grabs Dexter's harness, commanding him to get up. "Who's Sarah?" I ask, feeling out of the loop.

"You met her a few months ago," Charlie says. "At the bar? She was there with Mouse. She's Mouse's wife."

Mouse. I remember Charlie taking some time off last year when he died. She'd been devastated.

"I hate to run, ladies, but I'm her labour coach. I got a baby on the way!" she squeals, then rushes out onto the sidewalk.

I check my watch and realize that I really should go too. Bryce will be home from school soon, and I have to prepare myself to deal with Paul.

Jase

I CHECK MY watch and realize it's almost three o'clock. I place the hammer on the new customer service desk I've been building and call out to the guys. "I've gotta get outta here."

"Where's the fire?" Reaper calls from his spot on the ladder. He's been working on the install of the new security system, and still has a lot to do.

"I need to get to Ellen's before that cocksucker does. He's coming to pick up Bryce, and Bryce doesn't wanna go," I explain as I pull my cut back on and move towards the door.

Reaper takes a step down the ladder, his eyes on mine. I notice we've got the other guys' attention too. "You need backup?"

The truth is, I don't know. I don't know how I'm gonna deal with this asshole when he shows up. Ellen had tried to get a hold of him, but he hadn't answered his phone. I can't kick this guy's ass with Ellen and the kid standing right there. Maybe having a couple of the guys there will scare him off.

"Actually, that might be kinda perfect. As much as I want to beat this prick into the ground, Ellen and Bryce are already tweaked enough. It would scare the shit out of them. But the guy's a pussy, hiding behind the law. A little intimidation might be just what he needs."

"Whatever you say, man," Reaper says with a smirk and climbs down off the ladder.

Tease, Bosco, and Hulk put down their tools and follow me out to our bikes. We make the drive in record time, pulling up in front of the house just as Paul's getting out of his truck. I step off my bike; my eyes pinned on him where he stands, seemingly frozen on the spot.

"Your lead, VP," Reaper says low enough that Paul can't hear.

I flick my eyes up to the house and see Bryce watching from the living room window, his mother trying to pull him away. He doesn't budge. I can feel the weight of his stare as I walk towards his father, my boys right behind me.

"Window," Tease warns.

"I see him."

I can physically see Paul's Adam's apple slide up and down as he swallows, his eyes flicking from me to the others. His face is ashen, but he stands up a little straighter, his fists balled at his sides.

"Paul, glad I caught ya," I say as I step between him and the front door.

"I'm just here to pick up my kid, man."

I purse my lips and tilt my head to the side. "Yeah, about that. Your kid tells me that he doesn't wanna go."

Paul's face twists with anger. "I've got a court order—"

"Court orders don't mean shit," Tease sneers over my shoulder.

Paul looks to me and I shrug. "He's right. Bryce tells me you weren't all that nice to him on his last visit, Paul." I take a step forward. "You care to explain that?"

"Fuck that," he spits. "The kid's full of shit."

I take another step forward, and can feel the angry energy radiating off the guys behind me. "He also informs me that you called him a pussy. Does that sound like bullshit to you too, Paul?"

Paul throws his arms up and shakes his head. "Jesus Christ. What the fuck is it to you how I talk to my kid? Let me have my son, or I'm calling the police to report Ellen for breaching a court order."

Another step puts me right in his personal space. "Not gonna happen, Paul." Every time I say his name, I say it like a curse, and I smile inside when I see his anger go up another notch. "See, Bryce means something to me, and if he feels like he doesn't want to see you anymore, then he's not gonna see you anymore. You can call the cops if you'd like, but I gotta warn ya," I motion to the angry group of men behind me. "We don't like cops very much."

Paul's angry glare moves from me to over my shoulder, and I'm not sure exactly what he sees, but if Tease's shoulder bumping up against mine is any indication, I'm willing to bet he doesn't look too happy with Paul right now, and that's enough to scare anybody. Paul's face pales even more, and I can practically see the moment his balls crawl back up inside of him.

"I'll tell you what, Paul." I reach out and clamp my hand down on his shoulder, squeezing it until I see him flinch. "If Bryce changes his mind, I'll be sure to let you know, but in the meantime, you need to disappear. Yeah?"

Paul's eyes drift over my shoulder and up towards the house, and I know he's looking at Bryce. "Eyes off the kid," Tease growls, pressing against my back.

"Let me tell you what you're gonna do," I say. "You're gonna climb back into your fancy truck, and you're gonna get the hell out of my sight. You're not gonna call the cops, Paul, and you know why?"

He gulps loudly.

"'Cause even if they cart me off, these guys here won't like that either. There are about twenty-five more of us back at the clubhouse that wouldn't like it either." I point my finger and press it into his chest. "Now disappear."

Paul turns and hurries back to his truck, glancing back several times to make sure we're not following him. Once inside, he starts it up and peels out of the driveway. He's gone in an instant.

I look up at the house and see Ellen standing there, her hand on Bryce's shoulder. She smiles at me, but it's Bryce I'm looking at.

His face is solemn as he stares back, and simply nods before moving away from the window.

Poor kid.

Ellen

I watch from the window as Jase says goodbye to the others and wait for him to come inside. When I hear the front door open, I hurry to it and jump into his arms.

"Thank you," I whisper, emotion overwhelming me. Since this whole court thing started, Paul's behaviour has been unpredictable and terrifying. I'd been worried that this whole situation would end up being a grizzly news story on the eleven o'clock news.

Jase grasps my face in his hands, and presses a kiss to my lips. "No need to thank me, baby. Just glad he's gone." He looks around. "Where's B?"

"He went to his room after Paul left. I think he was upset."

"Of course he was."

I look at Jase in shock. "El, the kid's dad is a total douche. His mother's boyfriend just sent him packin' before his eyes, and the guy left without a word, making him a douche *and* a pussy. That kid's head is all kinds of confused right now."

I glance down the hall at Bryce's closed door, and rake my fingers through my hair. "God, I hate this! Raising a kid is hard enough, but there's no rule book on how to handle this kind of situation. I'm so afraid I'm messing this up."

"Not possible," he declares. "You love that kid, and he knows it. That's why he can afford to be such a miserable little prick to you sometimes, but he'll figure it out. He has you to help him, and me if he needs it."

"You know an awful lot about kids, and how to get through to them."

He presses a kiss to my forehead. "That's 'cause up until a few weeks ago, I think I was still one myself."

Jase turns, and I watch as he walks down the hall and taps a knuckle against Bryce's bedroom door. "Hey, B. Can we talk?"

Bryce's muffled voice carries down the hall, then Jase steps inside, closing the door behind him. I slowly walk down the hall, but I don't hear anything coming from the room. I consider approaching and listening from outside, but somehow that just feels wrong right now. Somehow, with barely knowing him, Jase seems to be more in tune with my kid than I do, and instead of making me feel jealous, I feel grateful. I trust that whatever Jase is saying in there is exactly what Bryce needs to hear.

I wander into the kitchen, my ears straining to hear Bryce's door open. I pull out the vegetables, cutting them up to make the salad, then move on to prepping the chicken to go into the oven. Finally, I hear the door creak open, and after a few seconds, Jase and Bryce are standing in the doorway.

"Hey, babe. Just grabbin' a beer, then B and I are gonna play a little Call of Duty. That okay?"

My heart soars when I see the way Bryce is looking up at him. The admiration I see in his eyes in something I've never seen from him. "Yeah," I choke out, trying to fight back the tears I feel creeping out. I'm just so glad that my boy is okay.

"Hey, Bud. Why don't you go get it set up? I need to talk to your mom for a second, okay?"

Bryce nods and runs out, no doubt jumping over the back of the couch, excited to be playing his favorite game.

"You okay, El?" Jase asks, his face full of concern.

I smile and pull a beer out of the fridge. "Fine."

He frowns and approaches me, pulling me into his body. "You sure?"

I nod and swallow back the lump in my throat. "He's not comin' back, babe. That fucker is gonna be having nightmares about Tease's ugly mug for months. He's not gonna risk pissin' any of us off, especially Tease."

I mentally picture Paul running from Tease in fear. "Well, you'll have to thank Tease for me."

He snags his beer from my hand. "You good?"

"I'm good."

"Good."

I watch his back until he's almost out of the kitchen, and call out, "Jase?"

"Yeah babe?"

"Thank you for taking care of my son."

"Always, babe. For both of you." With that, he turns and goes to play a video game with my son, who adores him, leaving me there to beat back the overwhelming emotion of realizing that I'm not falling in love with Jase Matthews—I already am.

Twenty-Three

Jase

I LOOK AROUND at the new garage and can't help but smile. This place is everything I've ever wanted, and in just a few weeks, it'll be up and fully operational. I've even got a few interviews set up next week for new mechanics. We'll be pumping out custom choppers like nobody's ever seen before.

The guys and I had spent the entire day here again today, working on the showroom and moving in all the equipment from the old place back at the compound. It's all coming together.

My phone alerts me to an incoming text.

Ellen: Hey you.
Me: Hey, baby. How's work?
Ellen: Good. On my break right now. Just wanted to tell you that Bryce is really excited you're coming to his game.

I grin. What can I say? The kid loves me.

Me: Me too. Just getting ready to go now.
Ellen: I was thinking that maybe you could spend the night to-night? That is, if you want to ;)

I swear my dick does a happy dance. Since all that shit with Paul went down the other night, Bryce hasn't left my side. We'd spent the entire weekend together, just the three of us. Well, I spent most of my time playing video games with Bryce. He went to bed at a decent time, but Ellen was terrified that he'd catch us in the act, and she wasn't ready for me to spend the night when he was home, so I'd been out the door by midnight, without getting any action at all.

Me: You ready for that?
Ellen: I was always ready ;) It was Bryce I was worried about.
Me: Can we put him to bed early?

I can picture her on the other end, rolling her eyes.

Ellen: Good things come to those who wait.
Me: If I wait any longer, my balls will burst.
Ellen: You're terrible. Wish my kid luck for me ☺

I have to smile, knowing exactly what annoyed tone she would have used if we were talking. Stuffing my phone back into my pocket, I take a final look around before turning off the lights, step-ping outside and pulling the door shut. With a turn of my key, the door is locked, and I'm ready to go.

I'd parked my bike on the far side of the lot to make room for the moving trucks we'd been using earlier today. I check my watch and realize that if I'm gonna make it to Bryce's game on time, I'd better haul ass. Traffic at this time of day is always a bitch in the city.

I'm just reaching for my helmet when the loud roar of a vehicle hits my ears. I turn just as a black Escalade screeches to a stop be-hind me. The passenger door swings open, and my eyes are level with the barrel of a gun.

I put my hands up as I look into the eyes of the man screaming for me to get down on the ground. Colt stares back at me, his eyes still filled with so much hate.

I drop to my knees, my mind racing as I try to think of a way out of this mess. From the corner of my eye, I see another guy open the back door of the SUV, and I turn to look in his direction. That's when everything goes black.

Ellen

The phone at the nurse's desk rings just as I'm finishing up my final rounds. I rush forward to get it, knowing my supervisor gets angry if it rings more than three time.

"B unit," I say, a little out of breath.

"Ellen, I have your son's school on line three. They said that nobody came to pick him up after his basketball game."

My stomach twists in a painful knot. "Put them through."

I take the call from the school, my heart racing as I assure them that I'll be right over to pick him up. I disconnect the call and press the extension number for my supervisor, letting her know that there's been an emergency, and I need to get to the school. Since my shift is almost over, she hurries down to take my place.

While grabbing my stuff, I call Jase's phone, my heart sinking when it rings a few times and goes straight to voicemail. I hang up without leaving a message and dial the only person I know that can help.

"Charlie, I think there's something wrong with Jase."

"What?" she gasps out. I can hear Ryker talking in the background before he gets on the line. "What's goin' on, sweetheart?"

"Jase never showed up for Bryce's basketball game," I blurt out. "The school just called and said no one showed to pick him up."

Ryker curses. I hear him talking to someone, giving orders, and then he's back on the line. "You at work?"

"Yeah." Tears burn my eyes as I try to keep it together. What could have happened to Jase? I know he wouldn't have missed that game for anything. It meant too much to him that Bryce had asked him to come.

"Reaper will be out front in ten, and I'm sending Tease to get your boy. You need to call the school and let them know he's coming. His real name is Travis Hale. They'll be bringing you both back to the clubhouse until we can figure out what the fuck is going on."

Ryker disconnects before I have a chance to respond. With shaking hands, I dial the school back and let them know that Travis Hale is a family friend, and that he'll be picking Bryce up. They don't agree right away, not until I explain that there's been an emergency. Finally, the principal takes pity on me and agrees to release my son to Tease.

Reaper is there before the ten minutes are up, and I jump onto the back of his bike without a word. The ride feels like it takes forever, my mind going over all of the possible scenarios of what could have happened.

We pull up to the clubhouse, and I look around for Bryce. "They're not here yet," Reaper grumbles. "Tease's ride isn't here. Come inside and I'll grab you a beer."

Feeling helpless, I follow him in, desperately praying that Ryker has something to tell me. Charlie and Ryker come out of the back hall, both of them looking grim. "Okay," Ryker says. "We used the Find My Phone app to locate Jase's cell, and we managed to find it. We'll wait for Tease to get back, then we'll go get our boy." His eyes move past me and he looks to Reaper. "The fuckin' Crips, man. It's gotta be. He's right in the middle of their territory."

"You call Jasper?" Reaper's voice is filled with anger.

"He says he knows nothin' about it. Thinks it might be that Colt kid. He's givin' us a free pass into the area to pull him out."

I look back and forth between them, not having the first clue as to what they're talking about. "Jasper? Colt? What's going on... where's Jase?"

Charlie comes forward and wraps her arms around me, while Ryker places his heavy hand on my shoulder. "We'll get him back, Ellen. You have my word."

Tease comes in with an excited Bryce. "Mom, that was awesome! Tease drove so fast! Jase never went that fast when we rode."

Tease smirks and winks at him, then looks at me and his head jerks. "Sorry, Mom," he drawls.

I don't get a chance to respond before every man in the room disappears, all of them going to wherever it is to "pull him out." I don't know what the hell is going on, but my heart is racing so fast, it feels as if it's going to explode.

I stand frozen in place, my eyes on the door. I can vaguely hear Charlie showing Bryce the pool table, and then she's beside me, her arm going around my waist. "Ryker will find him, Ellen. He loves him too."

I look up at her with tears falling from my eyes. I never told him that I love him.

Twenty-Four

Jase

THE SOUND OF two men arguing slowly pulls me from the hazy fog that I'm trying so hard to claw my way out of. My head swims and lolls around on my neck as I try to lift it. What the fuck happened to me?

"Jasper fuckin' knows, man! If he finds out I helped you start this shit, he'll fuckin' kill me right after he kills your crazy ass."

Groaning, I try to peel my eyelids apart and see where the hell I am, but they're not cooperating.

"You can't leave, you stupid fuck. He already knows. We need to finish this shit and get the hell out of here."

Colt. That last voice was Colt. He'd pulled up behind me when I was going to my bike. Then he'd clubbed me upside the head with the butt of his gun. That fucker is dead.

"You can't just kill the VP of a goddamn motorcycle gang, Colt. Especially not the Kings of Korruption. Those fuckers will come for you. You'll be dead before you even make it out that door."

"Those fuckers killed my brother," Colt roars. "They showed up, uninvited, to that deal. They mowed down the Crips, right along with those other bikers, and my brother was one of 'em! Did anybody do anything about that?"

"We killed their fucking Prez, man, and look where that got us. They killed everyone that was involved, including our leader. If we kill this asshole, nothing's gonna get solved. It'll only get worse."

"Whatever," he sneers. "Run home, ya pussy. I'm gonna show this asshole that the Kings don't run the fuckin' show around here."

I manage to open my eyes just enough to see the back of the guy Colt's been arguing with, run out the door. I look around through narrow slits and see myself in a shitty apartment, with concrete walls and wooden slat flooring. I'm sitting against the wall, my arms tied behind my back, which explains why they're numb. The rope used to tie them is cutting into my flesh, and I'm surprised I still feel them at all.

"I know you're awake, VP." I can practically hear his lip curl. "That's good, because we don't have very much time. Somehow, Jasper found out you're here, and he's on his way to kick my ass for fuckin' with you." He presses the barrel of the gun into the centre of my forehead. "Too bad for him, by the time he gets here, you'll be dead, and I'll be long gone."

I say nothing, because I can't. There's a filthy rag tied across my mouth. Colt's body shakes, causing the gun to vibrate against my skin. Discreetly, I struggle with the bindings on my wrist, but they're so tight, I can't move them, not even a little.

Sweat drips from my brow, trickling into my eyes as I survey the room, desperate to find a way out of this. My heart races as Colt's thumb moves to the hammer and slowly draws it back with a click.

Visions float through my mind, my gut twisting in despair. Ellen blinking up at me, her eyes full of emotion the night that I got rid of Paul. Bryce laughing over at me while I curse at the TV when I get slaughtered, yet again, in Call of Duty. Those two have come to mean so much to me in such a short amount of time. I can't let this fucker steal my family from me. I haven't even had the chance to love them yet.

Colt's finger tightens on the trigger. I squeeze my eyes closed, my breathing laboured and fast. Knowing that this is my only hope, I pull back my foot as fast as I can, and drive it up into Colt's chin. The gun in his hand never goes off.

I climb to my knees, trying like hell to get to my feet. But just as I do, Colt raises his gun. "Fuck you, asshole." He pulls the trigger.

Just as the gun goes off, the door to the apartment bursts open, and there they are. If I was a movie producer, I couldn't have staged it better myself. Colt swings around with his gun, ready to shoot again, but Tease beats him to it, placing a bullet directly between his eyes.

My body sways before I fall to my knees. "Jesus Christ," Reaper shouts. "Get me my bag!"

Reaper rushes over, lowering me to the ground, his face tense and his eyes wild as he yanks the gag from my mouth. "'Bout time you fuckers showed up." My voice is slurred, and I don't know why. "Hey, what's wrong?"

"You got a bullet in your belly, asshole. Would you just lay back and let me fuckin' fix it?"

I do as he says. The room spins as I lift my head from the floor, trying to see my stomach, but all I see are spots. Spots everywhere. "Hey Reap?"

Reaper presses something down against my stomach. "Yeah?"

"You gonna admit I got shot this time?"

Reaper curses and wraps his hand around the back of my neck, his face set in stone as he stares down at me. "You live through this, buddy, and I'll admit anything you want."

I close my eyes and let sleep carry me away.

Ellen

The guys have been gone for over two hours now, and nobody's heard from them at all. Bryce's fear had gotten the better of him since they'd left, and Laynie had found him crying in the bathroom a little while ago. He didn't want me to see him upset, so she'd distracted him with Dexter, asking him to keep the dog company. It's seemed to help so far, but every time someone walks in that door, I see the look of hope on his face and know that it likely mirrors my own.

An endless flow of people have been trickling into the common room of the clubhouse. Family members, old ladies, and even a few kids, all of them worried about Jase. They've been a wonderful support, and as I look around, I finally see the family dynamic that Charlie has told me so much about.

I'm refilling my coffee cup when the door swings open, banging loudly against the wall. I turn to see who it is, and my coffee cup falls from my hand, spilling coffee everywhere as the cup shatters when it hits the tile floor. Reaper and Tease enter the room, their arms both wrapped around Jase, who's walking between them, his feet dragging across the floor. Blood stains their hands and clothes, and Jase seems barely conscious.

They're moving fast, barreling through the room, and straight for the hall that leads upstairs. I stare in horror as one by one, the men file inside, all of their faces set in grim masks. "Wait!" I cry, running to catch up. Nobody stops. "Jase!"

Just as I enter the hallway, Ryker grabs me from behind. "Ellen, you need to wait out here."

I blink up at him, my heart sinking. "Is he okay?"

Ryker gives a single shake of his head, and for the first time, I notice the fear in his eyes. "But he will be. I'll let you know when I know more." With that, he turns and stalks off down the hall and up the stairs, leaving me staring after him. My entire world feels like it's crumbling down around me.

My eyes swing to Bryce, who's standing across the room, staring at me with his fists scrunched up into tiny balls at his sides. A tear slides down my cheek. Bryce breaks from his stance and runs full out, his body crashing into mine and knocking me back a step.

My heart breaks when I wrap my arms around his trembling shoulders as he lets out an agonized sob. "Please let Jase be okay," he cries.

Tease appears at the door. "Charlie?"

I watch as Charlie gives me a sad smile and disappears down the hall with Tease. I hold my son close, trying to soothe him. I move to the couch, where Bryce curls up against me, and I stare off into space, toying with his hair as we wait. We wait for over an hour before Charlie places a hand on my shoulder, pulling me back to the present.

"You can come up now," she says. "He's asking for you."

Bryce pops up beside me. "Can I see him, too?"

Charlie smiles. "He's asking for you too."

We follow Charlie up the stairs and enter, what I'm assuming, is Jase's room. He's lying shirtless in the centre of the bed, a large bandage on his side. His skin is pale, and I can smell the blood in the air. The door closes quietly, leaving me, Bryce, and Jase alone in the room.

Jase looks up at us and doesn't say a word. He just holds out both arms, motioning for us to come to him. As one, Bryce and I move to the bed, carefully climbing on each side of Jase and nestling up against him. I feel him press a kiss against the top of my head, then look up to see him do the same to Bryce.

Bryce looks up at him, his head on Jase's shoulder. "Are you okay?"

The dark circles under Jase's eyes worry me, and I press my hand to his cheek, satisfied that he doesn't seem to have a fever. He looks at Bryce and pulls him closer. "I am now."

"What happened?"

"I got shot," Jase says, a small smirk playing on his lips.

"For real this time?" Bryce asks, and I shake my head as he bites back a smile.

"Yeah, smartass. For real this time." He looks to me and rolls his eyes. "Geez. What a man gotta do to get some respect around here?"

I stare up at him, my throat burning as I think of how close I came to losing him. A sob bursts from my lips and I bury my face in his neck. "Hey," he soothes. "I'm okay, El. I'm okay."

"I'm not," I cry. Jase holds me close and presses soft kisses to my face and lips, waiting until the tears start to fade. "It's not okay, Jase. You scared the shit out of me. I've spent years keeping people out, and finally you come along, making me fall in love with you. Then you just disappear. You were gone! And then the blood, and nobody telling me anything, and me and Bryce, we were both—"

"Babe," Jase cuts in. "Slow down. It's over now." I sigh and my entire body relaxes against him, careful not to touch the place where his bandage is. "I love you too, El."

I pop up and stare at him with wide eyes, just as Bryce lets out a disgusted, "Gross."

"You do?"

"Baby, I think I've loved you from the moment you told me off that night at the club."

I blink at him and feel the bed move as Bryce climbs out. "I'm gonna go get a drink," he says as he walks to the door. Just before Bryce pulls the door closed, Jase calls out, "Hey, B?" Bryce pauses and looks back in. "I love you too, Bud."

Bryce grins, his face lighting up as he shakes his head and walks out.

When Jase's eyes move back to mine, my heart flutters in my chest. "You love me?"

Jase chuckles softly and pulls me closer. His lips hover above mine when he whispers, "I love you, El."

His lips cover mine in a kiss that warms me to my toes. It's soft, slow, and gentle. He kisses me in a way that will never again make me doubt the way he feels about me. He kisses me in a way that tells me, right down to my soul, that Jase Matthews loves me.

"I love you, too."

Jase

SUPPER," ELLEN CALLS from the kitchen. I put down the box I'm carrying inside and move in that direction. The house is filled with the delicious aromas of her cooking.

I walk into the kitchen and see Ellen and Bryce, both already seated at the round table, with an extra place between them that's meant for me. Watching Ellen spoon a helping of homemade macaroni and cheese onto Bryce's plate, my throat gets thick with emotion. All my life, I'd never had a home like this, or even many home cooked meals, and that had never bothered me. Looking back, I realize just how much I'd missed out on growing up the way I did. I'd never change my life for anything, but looking at my family, I realize that it only gets better from here.

"Come," Ellen says, reaching for the empty plate that's meant for me. "Sit. You must be hungry."

I shake off my thoughts and move to the seat between them. "Starved. I have one more trip to get the last of my stuff, but I think I'm pretty much moved in."

Concern crosses her face, and I don't miss her glancing down at my stomach. "Maybe you should leave the rest for tomorrow. You're still healing."

I smile and reach over, running my thumb across her cheekbone. "Don't worry, babe. I already planned to."

She smiles. "Good. It's only been two weeks. You don't want to overdo it."

I'd been lucky. The bullet from Colt's gun had entered the side of my abdomen, and gone straight through. It hadn't hit anything major, and between Reaper and Charlie, they'd been able to patch me up. It still hurts like a son of a bitch, but I don't complain. Every time I do, Reaper gives me a hard time about taking it like a man. Like that's an issue.

I eat my supper with a smile on my face, listening to Bryce talk a hundred miles an hour about his basketball tournament he'd gone to on Friday. I'd been there for it, but his mother hadn't, so I relive it again through his words, and love every second of it.

Bryce and I have become good buddies. He comes to me when he needs something, and I help him work it out. He teases me and I let it slide, sometimes getting in a dig or two of my own. Almost every night, we play a few rounds of Call of Duty, and last night, I'd finally killed the little shit three times. He tried to pass it off as beginner's luck, even though I've been playing it with him for weeks.

Paul hasn't made any attempt to contact Ellen or Bryce since our little conversation on the front lawn. I think Bryce has finally come to terms with the fact that his father's absence is for the best, realizing that the guy is just an asshole, and he's better off without him. Luckily for Ellen, she got her second child support payment, and whether she'll admit it or not, it's a huge help to her financially.

I unpack a few more boxes after supper, and I'm just finishing up in the bedroom when Bryce comes in. "You ready to watch a movie?"

"Yeah, Bud. Let me grab a beer and I'll be in."

I follow him out and grab a beer from the fridge before moving to the couch beside Ellen. "So, what are we watching?"

"The new Poltergeist," Bryce says with a smirk as he flicks

through the Netflix menu, trying to find the movie.

I let my head fall back on the couch. "Jesus Christ, B. Not you too."

He giggles and presses play, coming to sit on the couch on the other side of me. "I love scary movies."

I glare at Ellen and shake my head. "The evil woman has an evil son."

Ellen throws her head back and laughs. I watch her face as she does, and my heart swells. I love the sound of her laugh, and the way her eyes light up when she does. "Just watch the movie, ya big baby."

I turn back to the TV and shake my head. "Evil."

Ellen

The garage is deserted when the taxi pulls up, Jase's motorcycle being the only vehicle in the lot. I pay the driver and step outside. As he drives away, I look up at the new sign and smile. Korrupted Custom Choppers will be officially open for business tomorrow morning, and I'll be glad to get my man back.

Plans for the garage have been on hold since Jase had been shot, but now, more than two months later, there was no holding him back. For the past two weeks, Jase has spent every waking moment here, touching up the paint, changing out the sink in the bathroom, rearranging the tool shelves. The place looks incredible, and all his hard work is finally paying off.

I step inside and take in the shiny new chopper displayed in the centre of the floor. It's the only chopper on display right now, but it's gorgeous, and I know that it won't be here for long. Jase and his new team of mechanics will have their work cut out for them to keep this showroom stocked with something to show.

"Babe," Jase says from the door to the garage.

I turn to him and smile. "Hey. I just came to see if you needed a hand with anything. Bryce went over to Jimmy's house after school and won't be home until later. I missed you."

He comes forward, pulling me into his strong arms and takes my lips in a hard, breathtaking kiss. My entire body hums as I grab onto his biceps and hold on tight. Pulling his lips away just enough, he whispers, "I've missed you too, El."

I smile and pull him back down to me, letting the scent of motor oil and leather overwhelm me. The smell that is Jase. I press my lips against his, my heart rate getting faster as the heat builds low in my belly. How I ever went four years without sex is a mystery to me. Two weeks without Jase, and I feel like I'm ready to blow.

His tongue slips inside my mouth, sliding against my own as his hand reaches up and cups my breast. I shiver as his thumb grazes across my nipple. I want his hands on my flesh, not my clothes. I pull away from him and take off my shirt, tossing it to the floor. His eyes flare as I reach behind to unclasp my bra, which I throw on top of my shirt.

"Jesus," he groans, his mouth closing in on the tight bud of my nipple. My knees buckle as I dig my fingers into his hair, pulling him even closer. Jase releases my breast and looks me in the eye, a grin crossing his face. "Wanna try somethin'?"

I barely hear him. My hands yank and pull at his belt buckle, trying to peel him from his clothes as quickly as I can. He laughs and pulls them off, then loses his shirt. There he stands before me— naked, tan, and beautiful.

"Take your pants off," he orders.

I do as I'm told, kicking my jeans into another pile on the floor as I watch his body like a predator spying on its prey. He moves to the chopper, swinging his leg over the seat, then leans back until he's in a semi-reclined position and motions for me to join him.

"I don't know if this is gonna work," I whisper as I slowly straddle his lap.

He grabs my hips and bites his lip as he slips a finger deep inside me. I sigh and drop my head to his shoulder. "It will, babe. Put your feet on the pegs."

I open my eyes and stare down at him as I place my feet in the right position, feeling him swipe his cock through my wet centre.

Finally, I feel him at my entrance, and he guides me down. I watch in awe as he stares back at me, his mouth open in a silent gasp, his breaths coming out in stuttered pants as I slowly lower myself down onto him.

Pleasure radiates through me as I sink lower and lower, until he's deep inside of me. Leaning forward, I slam my mouth down onto his, and hold onto his shoulders as he uses my hips to rock me back and forth, my clit sliding along his skin.

My body flushes until I feel like I'm on fire. I can feel it building already. I let his rhythm take over, and using the foot pegs, I pick up the pace and slam my hips against his, his cock hitting me in just the right spot.

Jase's skin flushes, his cheeks ruddy as he cups my breasts with both hands and leans up to taste them. His teeth sink into my nipple and I'm gone. Like an exploding volcano, my orgasm bubbles over, my whole body shaking uncontrollably.

I hear Jase curse and his cock pulses deep inside as he empties himself into me. I continue to rock my hips slowly, watching his face as I stare deep into his eyes. I slow to a stop when his knuckles graze my cheekbone, and he presses a soft kiss to my lips.

Pulling back, I smile at him and declare, "This place is now officially open for business."

Reaper

I push my way through the crowd, my eyes on her. Tease had told me she'd gotten her old job back, but I needed to see it to believe it. I finally step up to the bar, and when she turns to take my order, her eyes grow wide.

"What the fuck are you still doin' here, Anna?"

Her face pales. "I'm staying with Charlotte until——"

"Are you shittin' me?" I yell, my face twisted in disbelief.

She swallows and takes a deep breath. "I'm staying with Charlotte until I get enough money to get my own place."

I slam my hands down on the bar. "You stupid bitch. You have some balls coming back here after you fucked over your sister like you did."

Her chin juts out. "Charlotte forgave me."

I narrow my eyes. "Yeah, she forgave you. She forgave you too fuckin' easily. Your sister has a soft heart." Tears form in her eyes, and all it does is make me angrier. "I can't believe that Ryker agreed to let a whore like you stay in his home." Anna flinches as if I'd slapped her, but I don't stop. "If some toxic pussy tried to sell my old lady to pay off her credit card debts, I'd rip her fuckin' spine out of her asshole and piss on what's left. You need to go back to whatever hole you crawled out of, and never come back."

Anna squares her shoulders. "I'm not going anywhere, Reaper. Charlotte is giving me a chance to make things right, and I'm not going to leave just because you want me to."

I stab a finger at her, holding her eyes captive. "I want to make something perfectly clear here, woman. Skanky bitches like you are like poison to an MC. Ryker won't send you packin' because he loves his woman, but I won't stop until you're gone. I refuse to let you fuck up what we have here. Charlotte and Ryker are happy. You do anything to change that, you better pray I never get my hands on your scrawny ass. We clear, bitch?"

Anna's hand flits to the base of her throat, and a tear slips down her cheek. "I'm trying to change," she whispers.

"Whores never change," I spit out before I turn and walk out of the bar.

Watch Out For

Reaper

Book #4 in the
Kings of Korruption MC Series

Coming 2016!

About Geri

Geri Glenn lives in beautiful New Brunswick, Canada. She is an army wife, the mother of two gorgeous but slightly crazy little girls, and just recently is fortunate enough to quit her day job to stay home and do what she loves most - write!

Geri has been as avid reader for as long as she can remember. When she isn't writing or adulting in some other fashion, she can usually be found curled up in a comfy chair, reading on her iPad both day and night. Geri is an incurable night owl, and it's not uncommon for her to still be awake, reading at 4 am, just because she finds it hard to put the book down.

Geri loves all genres of fiction, but her passion is anything romantic or terrifying; basically, anything that can get her heart pumping. This passion has bled out onto her laptop and become the Kings of Korruption.

Writing that first book in the series has knocked off the #1 thing on Geri's bucket list, and publishing it has been an absolute dream come true. She hopes you love the Kings as much as she does.

Stalk her!

♛ Facebook: https://www.facebook.com/geriglennauthor

♛ Twitter: https://twitter.com/authorgeriglenn

♛ Instagram: https://instagram.com/authorgeriglenn/

♛ Website: http://geriglenn.weebly.com/

CPSIA information can be obtained
at www.ICGtesting.com
Printed in the USA
LVOW10s0253101017
551850LV00025B/1049/P

9 781530 867899